A GALLE

She had led him off to the spare room upstairs – which was very considerate of her. He was kneeling with his back to me as I entered, his face pressed against her navel. She sat, naked to the waist, on the high four-poster, with an arm around his bull neck. She took no notice of me whatsoever, and her conquest, oblivious of all else but the free gift of this magnificent body, did not even hear me come in.

He had evidently set about his business without a second's hesitation. The square, exaggeratedly masculine shoulders obscured her lower half from view, while his bent head was sunk in the hollow of her lap, and blindly, with both brown, hairy paws upstretched, he mauled, rather than fondled, Casilda's breasts. The way the fellow manhandled those sumptuous tits struck me as exceedingly uncouth for a Latin lover: he plucked and tugged at them like some famished urchin snatching oranges from a tree . . .

A GALLERY OF NUDES

Anthony Grey

A NEXUS BOOK
published by
the Paperback Division of
W. H. Allen & Co. plc

A Nexus Book
Published in 1987
by the Paperback Division of
W. H. Allen & Co. Plc
Sekforde House, 175/9 St. John Street,
London, EC1 4LL

Printed and bound in Great Britain by
Courier International Ltd, Tiptree, Essex

ISBN 0 352 32046 X

stickler for observing the customs of the country, oddly enough. He even subscribed to our ceremonial segregation of the sexes at the end of dinner: his guests had to linger over their port or brandy in the approved style. He had not gone so far as to emulate the Englishman's longing to dispense with the company of womenfolk entirely, although he had acquired the habit of brightening visibly as soon as the opposite sex were out of earshot. I meanwhile was cursing myself for having succumbed to the temptation of shocking Helen. What were they discussing now in their domains, I wondered? Surely Casilda would never be so tactless as to taunt our mutual friend about my piece of atrocious bad taste a moment ago? Ah, to hell with them. What did I care, anyhow. Lucien was not one to let his wife's dislikes interfere with a business deal that happened to take his fancy.

When we finally joined the ladies I was granted the privilege of exchanging platitudes with the highly scented Mme. Gomez-Garriga. Casilda, I was glad to note, ignored me completely. It was time, I felt, to end this happy evening, I rose to my feet. 'Don't go yet,' Lucien protested. 'Cassy, give Grey some whisky.' We met and hovered by the tray of drinks at the far side of the room. She was almost as tall as I. I saw her suddenly for the first time – the slender, supple body in the low-cut, shimmering, powder-blue sheath of an evening dress that seemed so cold and metallic, though it moulded her hips like a bathing suit and barely, precariously shielded her arrogant bosom; the

plain, chilly platinum band at her throat; the rich
tawny glint on each loose chestnut curl. She was
appetising in the extreme, it now dawned on me.
If this was Helen's playmate, then Helen was lucky.
A sleek young beast, full of surprise: an amalga-
mation of contrasts.

'Mostly soda,' I said. 'And plenty of ice.'

'Say when.'

'Tomorrow.'

'What's that? I don't get you.'

'An invitation.'

There was a loud splash, a clinking of ice against
glass, and silence. She did not look up.

'To luncheon or dinner,' I repeated. 'As you
wish.'

Damn the girl – still not a word. She might have
been stone deaf.

At last 'Is that how you like it?' she asked,
without interest.

'Yes, fine, thanks,' I answered, sipping my drink.

Casilda shrugged her naked shoulders. 'I'll settle
for that one story,' she said. 'Tell me now.
Nobody's listening. Or do I have to accept your
hospitable suggestion and hear the whole saga of
your life?'

'Heaven forbid.'

'But you prefer to make it a bedtime story apparently, Mr Grey?'

I laughed. 'Certainly not,' I assured her. 'I've
never mentioned it to a soul until tonight.'

'I'll think it over – if I may.'

CHAPTER ONE

It was not a big dinner party that night at the Delavignes'. There were eight of us, all told – an awkward number to seat. Disliking Lucien as I do, I might easily not have accepted Helen's invitation. As a rule it was an honour that I made a habit of declining, although I did a fair amount of business with the Baron Delavigne. On this occasion I believe there were a couple of pictures which I hoped to persuade him to buy – a Guardi and a Zubarán, if I am not mistaken. Probably that was why I came to be dining at his house in Regent's Park. Only the year before last – and yet how immensely long ago it seems!

The fare itself was excellent, I must admit. And the wines too, as usual. Lucien has supremely good taste in everything. Helen, for instance, is a show-piece: one of his finest possessions. Although he had tired of her long since, and made no secret of it, even his exorbitant pride must have revelled in the thought that he owned such a dazzling beauty for a wife. Helen is not exactly my type – but she was looking wonderful that evening, and no two ways about it. Dark, pale, fragile, superbly *soignée*, she had that genuinely cultured yet peculiarly humourless mentality of the extremely well-bred American. Perhaps she would have appeared more admirable in Boston than in London.

Despite Lucien's arrant cynicism and physical coarseness, in many respects they were a well-matched couple. Taut and distraught as she was beneath that elegant surface, I feel sure that Helen still derived the utmost satisfaction from her successful marriage to a member of the French aristocracy. She enjoyed his title, their smart town house, their distinguished guests, her socially eminent position in the art world – for she had a foot firmly planted in both camps, and more than anything she resembled the graceful equestrienne daintily straddling the broad backs of a pair of stolid horses at the circus. By the matriarchal instinct of her American upbringing, as a good hostess and a convinced feminist, she had not relinquished her lawful place at the head of Lucien's table. I was on her left, with her handsome young friend Casilda Vandersluys between me and some dismal diplomat, a wealthy Argentine or Venezuelan, I vaguely remember.

At the corner diagonally across from mine, where Lucien sat, the conversation sparkled with that

6

have lamentably neglected to satisfy their natural feminine desire.

Not just one wench in heat, but a pair, a couple of women's bodies locked in the throes of passion – the very thought of it excites and fascinates me (providing of course that neither partner in the frolic is old, ugly or too masculine to arouse my lecherous envy). Each of them kneels at the same shrine as I, and as a spectacle it always thrills me, for the multiplication of their charms doubles my lustful impulse to give the crazy bitches a taste of the real thing. If I set my mind to it, I am confident that I can wean them away from their pointless preference – or at any rate I can usually break up the affair by enticing the one I want back to normal. Fortunately, genuine, dyed-in-the-wool lesbians are rare, for they tend to appeal to the natural instincts of a proper man as laughably little as either type of male pervert – the murky-eyed bugger or the simpering bumboy. Sappho, in that setup, wears the trousers. She is an even greater menace than the ordinary husband she apes and would give a good few years of her life to be. Husbands, after all, have been known to see reason, nobly overcoming the cruelest pangs of jealousy. But not the female homosexual. Scorned, she is, as ever, deadlier than the male. Beware of her vengeful claws – but lure her dreamy little wife away from her just the same. It can be done with patience, skill and care – like prising certain spiky kinds of seafood off a rock.

This train of thought did not enter the crowded,

smut-begrimed station of my mind – nor even flash through it, I swear – during that dull, yet eventful dinner at the Delavignes'. In the whole of an existence devoted mainly to the keen pursuit of pleasure, I have seldom been less conscious of an intriguing opportunity. The brain and the heart, no less than the flesh itself, frequently let one down in such cases, I have discovered. Be that as it may, I can truthfully assert that I was not, at the time, in the least concerned or curious about any amorous relationship that our handsome hostess might have established with her dear friend on my left.

Helen I admired for her good looks, her social gifts, her poise; but she meant almost as little to me, I confess, as the plump and merry Mme. Gomez-Garriga across the table. And if I went out of my way to be affable with Casilda Vandersluys, it was chiefly in order to pass the time of night as congenialy as possible. I had no designs on her person. My only ulterior motive, if any, was of a more sordid kind: there is never much harm in acquiring an extra ally at court. By the beginning of the third course I had contrived to glean several essentials facts about my charming neighbour.

She had lived with the Delavignes, on and off, for the best part of ten years – ever since her mother, a school friend of Helen's in Baltimore, had abandoned Casilda's father for a series of disreputable lovers. Or perhaps he had already left her by then. He was a Dutchman and a wastrel called Vandersluys, who had vanished without a trace at this stage, when Casilda was finishing her

10

education at Lausanne. Her mother, a hopeless alcoholic now, was seldom out of an inebriates' home. She herself had undergone two brief marriages, and after the second divorce had reverted to her maiden name. 'Aunt' Helen, as she then was to Casilda, and Lucien, the soul of kindness, had adopted her, so to speak, at the age of seventeen, when her parents separated on the brink of murder; and she had returned to them at intervals, whenever her life threatened to become unbearable. Not that she had ever sunk so low as to go crawling back to them for comfort, she was at some pains to assure me – but Helen 'just naturally seemed to be there, on hand when needed' (as I could well imagine) 'like a lifeboat in constant readiness to anticipate any signal of distress.' She received a small sum of alimony from her second husband, whom she had dismissed for 'persistent cruelty,' and her old Dutch grandfather, an East Indian planter who adored 'his little girl' (she shuddered at the phrase, as though accusing him by implication of incestuous tamperings with a minor), had left her a dwindling legacy which she scornfully described as 'conscience money.' She wrote fairly regularly for the fashion magazines and had done 'quite a bit of modelling' in her time (as also I could well believe).

'Mother is American-born,' she added, 'like me. She's of Hungarian, Irish and Scots extraction. So I suppose you'd say I'm a thorough mongrel. My paternal grandmother was slightly Eurasian – I think a quarter Javenese.' At this point the watchful

Helen intervened. I had monopolised Casilda too long, evidently. As a guest I was not pulling my weight – and I had hardly addressed a single remark to my hostess. I assume it was etiquette, rather than jealousy, that prompted her to cut in:

'I was just pointing out to Count Zwieburst that we're a perfect cocktail here tonight – if you go back a generation, I mean. Between us there are as many as nineteen nationalities represented around this table. Isn't that interesting? Lucien has some Polish blood, you know. Mr Grey is the only one of us – except, of course, Wagstaff – who is pure and unmixed. You *are* entirely English, aren't you, Anthony? And even he has lived most of his life abroad, I understand. Really you and Lucien ought to have switched birthplaces!' She ended with a gay, reproving little laugh.

'Yes, my home,' I said, 'if I had one, would be Paris.'

'But you were born in England, surely?' Helen inquired. 'I would describe you as more of a cosmopolitan than an expatriate.'

'I'd like to think so myself,' I answered. 'There was a time when you would have called me an exile. That's what I was. I fled the country – let me see – thirty years ago; and waited out of harm's way until any troublesome consequences were bound to have blown over.'

I was aware, as I spoke, that it was stupid and ill-mannered of me to tease Helen with this facetious reply. I have no idea what made me do it. But her air of superiority annoyed me, I wanted to ruffle her smug, grand-ladylike composure. And she should have had the sense to leave it at that, without provoking me to further indiscretions. Her butler and I were clodhoppers, were we? We were the only two dumb Englishmen in the company of her high-born foreign guests. Then why didn't she go on chatting with her wretched Count and leave me in peace? He was heavily engaged with half a partridge on his plate; perhaps he was a trifle deaf: he paid no attention to us. I had been quite happy talking to Casilda. That was just it, I expect. Foolishly, Helen chose to pursue the conversation.

'You make it sound as if you were wanted by the police for some terrible crime!' she exclaimed. 'But how thrilling!'

'I was. For indecent assault – with violence.' I informed her. (I was gilding the lily a bit; there had been no actual violence.) 'But in later years I've come to doubt whether they would ever have managed to pin it on me. The offence was committed by stealth. The circumstances were peculiar. Probably I'd have been safe enough, had I stayed. And yet – who knows? Somebody might have identified me, if the victim herself couldn't.'

Helen recoiled indignantly, as though I had leaned over and pinched her thigh. She glared at me for a second in utter amazement before plunging into small talk with the blissfully impervious Count. I could see her thinking: 'Anthony is drunk!' At that same moment I was conscious of Casilda's gaze, fixed inquisitively upon me from the side. I turned and smiled at her in apology – but whether

13

it appeared a sardonic or a sheepish apology, I cannot say. Her hazel eyes were twinkling and brimful of amusement.

'Explain the mystery to me, please,' she requested, so softly that it was almost a whisper. 'I simply don't follow. Did you blindfold the poor girl? Or strangle her with her stocking? No, I see – you bashed her on the head and knocked her out, is that it?'

I tried to talk of something else, I forget what.

'Tell me,' she insisted. 'I'm consumed with curiosity.'

'Come, I was only joking,' I said. 'And curiousity is both unhealthy and dangerous at your tender age.'

'Never mind. I am going to know. You can't refuse to answer – or I shall drag Helen into it again.'

'But you have already heard. As I told Helen, it was a – well, rather too great a liberty perpetrated on impulse. A case not of malice aforethought, you might say, but precisely the reverse. A stab in the dark.'

'How tiresome you're being! I still don't see what you mean.'

'No – I didn't intend you to. Let's drop the subject. Personally I'm entirely in favour of mixed marriages. I've known – '

But Casilda by now was hobnobbing intently with the gentleman on her left, the swarthy diplomat from Ecuador or Peru. We had been served a delectable cheese savoury. Lucien was a tedly I was twice her age, I reckoned – wrongly, for she was over twenty-five (in fact she was two years older than I guessed). Anyhow, what did that matter? Probably she was just as bored with these people as I was. My cherised reputation as an insatiable *roué* and expert ladykiller was not likely to worry her, for she seemed a sensible young woman, and must have realised that I took no particular interest in her from the mating point of view. Besides, if she did happen to belong to the rival persuasion (which I could scarcely credit; you never would have taken her for a lesbian – or at least not an authentic one), what difference could it make? Might we not be all the more agreeably at ease together? I for one would certainly not hold any queer little foible of that sort against her. As I worship and adore women, and every single lovely woman, on principle, if two of these heavenly creatures find delight in each other, I, a professed and eager sensualist can only wish them joy. Alas, I cannot myself fornicate with them all – not even with a tenth as many as I still could wish. Why then should I be so churlishly narrow-minded as to resent what some members of my sex deplore as a wicked waste of ecstasies which they consider they should be called upon to share? On the contrary, I would be the last to deny the ladies their innocent pleasure, while merely regretting that it is of necessity both limited and negative. Good luck to them! By all means let them solace their unfulfilled cravings as best they may, since my fellow men bright banality which one expects at politely convivial gatherings of this sort. It toyed with topics ancient or up-to-date, yet neither truly wise nor gay. Helen's splendid diamonds outshone a famous Italian soprano's broken shafts of wit. For myself, partly in desperation but largely from habit, I endeavoured to draw out the personality of my quiet, attractive neighbour – the American girl with the fair complexion and the exotic looks, whose place in the household I suspected of being more than simply that of an intimate friend of the family. I had met her briefly once before – that is to say. I had been introduced to her, wearing ballet tights, some weeks previously, when I had called round there one evening to talk business with Lucien. She had spectacles on her nose then, and seemed strangely aloof. Tonight she struck me as a good deal less forbidding.

Lucien had said: 'You know Casilda, don't you? A great friend of my wife's. She lives with us.' I noticed at the time that there was the hint of a leer in his voice, as though what he really meant was: 'They live together.' But one could never tell with Lucien. He often employed that sly tone when referring to Helen, as if to nudge you and confide: 'All the money is here, I suppose you realise. I married a very rich heiress.' So I thought nothing of it. We shook hands, and I went with Lucien into his study.

I had the impression now that Casilda and I were hitting it off pretty well, and this rather surprised me, although, of course, there was no earthly reason why we should fail to get on. Admit-

'By all means. I will telephone you one of these days to learn your decision.'

Her tone abruptly changed. 'No – please don't do that,' she begged. 'I would rather you didn't call me here. I will ring you.'

'Very well. But I won't promise to obey unless you contact me within the next week.'

'That's quite likely. I'm dying to hear this unrepeatable tale. I simply can't wait.' She grinned, to my astonishment, as though delighted to have pulled my leg. 'Good night, Mr Grey.'

It was too much, that twist. The mischievous, deceitful slut! What the devil was she playing at? I had not had the very slightest intention of seeing her again or taking her out to lunch – not seriously, anyway. I can't imagine what got into me. I didn't want the woman. Yet for the second time that evening I had made an ass of myself – a youthful, callow, incautious ass. At my age I ought to have known better. Bewildered and embarrassed, I watched Casilda walk away from where I stood, finishing my whisky. In that tight, shining prison of a grown her buttocks moved like a pair of wild animals pacing steadily back and forth across a cage. My, but how they stood up to the most searching scrutiny! They jutted out at you in marvellous, mocking challenge under your very nose. Hers was a body, not a 'figure'; it was built for the beach, the bath or the bed, not for clothes. The majestic action, the impudent, visible shape of her backside, its taut, inviting contours, the deep, dividing crack, the firm-fleshed, rolling spheres, sweeter than water-melons – you missed none of it. Too sallow for a blonde, her dark-brown hair of too light a tint to rate her a brunette, with those clear, perplexing hazel eyes that seemed to take on different shades as you gazed into them, she was – as she herself so rightly said – a thorough mixture. But by no stretch of the imagination was this the fluffy, soft, fey, feminine type that is most often apt to inspire a lesbian love.

Zwieburst offered me a lift home, but I insisted that it would be taking him out of his way and hailed a taxi, which I stopped in Belgrave Square for the pleasure of strolling through the mild September night to my small place in Chelsea. The fresh air would do me good. 'You're flushed with wine,' I told myself, wishing that the remonstrance were true. The fact was that Casilda disturbed and puzzled me. Not for many more years than I cared to remember had I experienced this unmistakable, obsessive, overwhelming tyranny. I had given up all hope – or fear – of succumbing yet again to the sexual infatuations of early manhood. Tonight I had gone to the Delavignes' in a mood of the purest innocence and boredom – but here I was now, suddenly trapped and ensnared. Only momentarily, I swore to that: I must put her right out of my mind by the morning.

I struck down to the Embankment. Not far from there – a couple of miles up river – was the scene of the crime, the huge office block where that lapse had occurred in my young days, when I had recently arrived in London. I was just over twenty.

It was midsummer. I went to fetch a former college friend of mine out to lunch. His office was on the top floor of a tall modern building that overlooks the Thames. He had forgotten our appointment, I discovered, for there was nobody in. His door was ajar, as he must have left it. I was scribbling a note for him at his desk when I heard strange sounds from the next room, where his secretary worked. I listened, and made out muffled cries for help. I went to look and an extraordinary sight met my eyes. At first I was at a loss to know what was happening. Miss Morley – Beryl, as I think he called her – was leaning on tiptoe, far out of the window. Both her shoes were off. Her feet hardly touched the ground. She may have been feeding crumbs to the birds or watering some potted plants on the ledge. But she was a prisoner, caught and held fast by the heavy frame, which had fallen across the small of her back. The sash-cord must have snapped. There she was, half-in and half-out of the room, pinned at the middle on the window-sill, unable to move.

No one was about. The other couple of offices on the same floor were empty; everybody else had gone out to eat. And the noise of the traffic below drowned her piteous calls for assistance. She would have to wait for an hour at least, until someone returned – and rushed to set her free. I glanced at my watch: 12:55. My first impulse was to spring to Beryl's rescue. But those hideous short, tight skirts of the period presented me with a vista so startling that I stopped dead in my tracks. I knew the girl to be a plain, unromantic specimen – young but mousy, with a shiny pink complexion and ginger hair. Seen from this angle, however, Miss Morley showed a marked, a most striking improvement. As stretch of stockinged leg, topped by garters, and a glimpse of bare thigh revealed to me hidden charms which I could never have suspected, but for this fortuitous and surprising encounter. In a position that was both provocative and comically undignified, she presented, in utter ignorance, an irresistible target. She was none other than Venus Calliope in person! Bless her beautiful bottom! I stood there for a moment, transfixed, enjoying the view to the full – and a full, firm, pleasant prospect it was: the great round moon veiled by clouds. Quickly and quietly I went back and shut all three doors, bolting the outer one. She had no idea, not an inkling, poor sweet, that there was somebody there. It gave her a start – what a start! – when I touched her. She jumped – though she could not budge, her backside leapt in the air, like a porpoise – when I slid my hand gently between her soft, fat thighs. She struggled violently, trying to turn her head, to see who it was that dared to caress her so intimately, so brazenly, and yet anonymously . . . I was quite safe: there was no chance of her recognising her unknown, unwanted (and perhaps unwarrantable) but far from unfriendly assailant.

Her response to my prying fingers was anything but calm, resigned or generous. She fought a fierce rearguard action, kicking out at me viciously with her heels. It was all she could do, though absurdly ineffective. With her tail tilted up towards me at that angle, her frantic attempts to press her legs together were quite useless, and however hard she strained, shrinking and closing her buttocks in a kind of frown, I would not remove my hand, so she might as well have abandoned any hope of dislodging it. I merely stepped aside and continued stroking her at my leisure. She was waving her arms wildly, like a signaller, and I suppose she redoubled her anguished shouts, but I did not bother to listen. I was much too intent on the task at hand. I myself made no sound; I scarcely breathed. With great difficulty I managed to tug her narrow, almost skintight skirt over her hips and roll it up neatly out of the way, exposing the smooth, ample panorama of her luscious behind, clad only vaguely in that unbecoming, silly garment known as cami-knickers, which women wore at the time. It was an obstacle all too easy to displace; that is the best you could say for it.

Now I could see what I was doing – and the sight of those rosy, rounded, twin spheres, that beauteous, broad map of the world, those glorious private bastions at the gates to inner joy, was as pleasing to the eye as was the satin-sleek feel of the pure flesh, the warm, furry cleft, the tender, chubby lips, to the touch of my exploring hands. But her savage efforts at self-defence continued. Her silken heels hacked ferociously though vainly, at my shins. There was nothing else for it: a ruler lay within reach on her desk, unluckily for Beryl's rump. She could not aim her furious kicks, whereas it was impossible for me to miss. Half a dozen peremptory strokes – not too hard, just by way of warning – were enough to quiet her down, after she had danced a lively little jig, with brightly blushing cheeks, for my exclusive benefit.

As soon as order had been restored by this brisk though not vindictive chastisement, I changed weapons, discarding the inflexible ruler for a more personal instrument of correction, specially designed for the purpose, as the bayonet is the arm to use when it comes to attacking at close quarters. Naturally, by this time, I was so eager for the fray I could restrain myself no longer. My aggressive instincts had been roused, for minutes on end, to the fullest pitch of enthusiasm – and in those far-off, happy days of bounding, abundant youth I was equipped with instantaneous and imperious reflexes that would brook no delay; the very last thing I could muster was patience or pity. Time was short; one o'clock had struck some while ago. I had a couple of open targets at my disposal. I reconnoitred them both for a moment or two with the tip of my sturdy thermometer – still in absolute silence, without a word or so much as a sound, not even a grunt. I spread the girl's protuberant buttocks apart with both hands and examined each orifice carefully, at some length – as also in depth – until I could stand this tantalising choice of objectives not another second, but at once lunged forward all the way into the further redoubt, lifting her up by her strong, wide hips as I did so, thrusting inwards with my palms to cushion the impact of my belly as it collided sharply with her pierced and battered fanny from below, while I rammed home my unfair advantage to its swift, speechless climax of convulsive rapture.

Raised in that position, like a wheelbarrow, with her feet off the floor, as though flying, yet gripped in mid-air and clamped on to me, almost sailing through space — but saved by the weight of the heavy wooden frame across her waist at the back — the mingled sensations and emotions that ran riot through her brain and body were not easy for a heartless male to fathom. All I know is that my own bliss was complete, though soon over. I was also greatly relieved, let me add, to find that she had not in fact been a virgin when I so rudely forced my attentions upon her. I thanked her for that, too, in my fashion — by kissing her fondly on both cheeks, and giving them a friendly pat, before I adjusted her dress, and fled. It was the least I could do to show my profound gratitude.

Perhaps there was no real need to worry — but something told me that I had been recognised, by the hall porter or an office boy, I could not be certain who it was exactly, as I hurried out of the building. This vague but alarming impression preyed on my mind; I took fright, as I admitted to Helen, and went abroad within the next thirty-six hours.

How could I have dreamed of recounting this singularly unedifying tale to a stranger? Whether it .shocked or amused her made no difference. I would be asking for trouble if I let myself get mixed up with Casilda. Fortunately, the question was unlikely to arise, however. Curiosity is a powerful snare, it's true, and Helen's handsome inamorata seemed to have swallowed the bait of my saucy story. That by itself was surely enough to indicate that she was not addicted to tribadism by nature but merely as a hobby. Still, we both had sound reasons for fighting shy of each other, I argued. There was precious little chance of my contriving to seduce Miss Vandersluys.

Yes, maybe so. I knew that I was right – yet the idea of wresting her from Helen excited me. I had sensed a challenge and, whatever the consequences, I already knew that I could not resist it. She had thrown down the gauntlet, and I must brace myself once again to give battle. I would defend my honour as a chartered libertine at all costs – and take a manly tilt at her. Confound the haughty half-caste houri! I was still capable of humbling her wanton's pride. We would see by what right she put on such superior sexual airs and graces.

The fresh night breeze blew cool in my face as I walked beside the river, but it did not clear the fevered confusion of my brain. Let me be strictly honest with myself, since I am writing this frank record of my private life for one person, above all, who knows me intimately. I was torn between two moods – exhilaration and despondency, self-assurance and fearful anxiety, optimism and a nagging presentiment of defeat. I strove to overcome the secret admission in my heart that Anthony Grey was not the man – the potent male, the rake, the

24

wolf, the stallion – that he had been until very lately. Don Juan's flamboyant, cocksure attitude was a bluff, a grinning, youthful mask to hide the wrinkled look of worry verging on despair. His boasts lacked conviction, as his limbs now had begun to lack vigour. His virility was approaching exhaustion. It was a sham – or at best, a matter of luck.

The change was recent, and I fought against it. Only a few months before I would have had no cause for alarm at the prospect of pitting my wits against Casilda's wiles; I would have popped her into bed without any of this miserable hesitation, I would have put her straightaway on her back and taught her a lesson, serving her as she deserved. But there had been too many failures – sad, shaming, inexplicable failures – since my previous birthday. I did not care to dwell on them. I was 'pushing fifty,' as the saying is. Muscles once supple were hardening, what had been stiff had grown limp; my body no longer obeyed me promptly and precisely at will. I could not, I dared not, rely on its performance. All too often it let me down at the crucial moment, giving rise only to mutual, meagre disappointment.

The memory of Mireille, for instance, was mortifying – and also the humiliation I suffered with little Joan. Veronica H. F. had been patient but puzzled, that ravishing redhead picked up on the Rome flight had insulted me, and sweet, darling What-was-her-name burst into tears. She was only nineteen. There were others, too – though I had scored some partial successes. It was not all over with me yet; I was certain of that. I had the proof in an occasional, wholly satisfactory response on their part. The slim, brandy-freckled maid at the hotel in Zurich had evidently enjoyed herself with a vengeance when I lugged her on top of me in my room; she came back for more, but the next time there wasn't any at first, until she had earned her fun. A willing worker. And the plump Danish trollop I met at a stifling cocktail scrum: she was too drunk to notice how little she amused me until later, after she had slept it off; then I could not get rid of her, she hollered for a repeat, sober, which of course was ineffectual, and called me a lot of rude names. . . .

I was not going to run the risk of any such disastrous scene with the sophisticated, derisive, intensely desirable Casilda. Slouched in my big armchair at home, clasping a tall glass of whisky that was the colour of her glowing, deep-golden skin, I brooded over this painfully personal problem far into the night. It was impossible – but I must have her. Peace would elude me until I had altered that faint smile on her lips to a different grimace. Could I still do this to a woman, as, and how, I wished? I had put a match to the logs in the grate, but already my fire was out. Too soon.

CHAPTER TWO

Days passed without a sign from Casilda Vandersluys. I felt offended, relieved, angry and glad by turns. It was just as well that my silly gaffe should be forgotten, and anyhow I had never expected her to ring me up, I told myself. She was really not in the least interested, for a start. There was nothing brazen about that young woman in either appearance or behaviour, so far as I could see – and obviously she was not so unwary a player as to lay herself open to a crushing snub or a lecherous pounce on the fully justified assumption that she was asking for it. I should have had to be a thousand times more courteous and more subtle if I was going to get anywhere with her. But since it had never been my intention to try my hand as a poacher on Helen's preserves, why was I now so acutely hurt and disappointed by Casilda's indifference? Surely I must remain equally aloof. It was a completely trivial incident, and it was closed.

A week went by, and still I could not banish that haunting, attractive ghost from my thoughts. She flitted through my dreams like an elusive nymph, whose image I was constantly remodelling in my mind's eye, as one always does in such cases. I longed to see her again, if only for a moment, to fix my changing impressions of the girl. I recalled her features and certain isolated details of her figure and expression, her walk, her unusual colouring, the sound of her voice, the serenely forceful impact of her calm personality. Yet she escaped my groping recollection of her portrait on the mental screen which we employ to recapture absent scenes and people, just as in reality she denied me the favour of her physical presence. It was not a blurred picture that I carried with me, but a reflection on the still waters of a lake, which a tossed pebble or a light gust of wind was enough to shatter.

I decided, against my better judgment, to disobey her strict injunction. I would telephone her at the Delavignes' – not immediately, but within the next few days. The effect of this decision was magical. It was as though I had rubbed Aladdin's lamp, summoning a genie on the line. The bell tinkled, and Casilda spoke. She had half an hour to spare that evening, thanks to a cancelled engagement. She supposed I would not be free, but if by any chance I was, and cared to receive a social call, she would drop by for a drink, towards 7:30. I asked if she knew my address before it occurred to me to put her off with some patently false excuse. That perhaps would have been the proper course, but I did not think of it until later. She said yes, she would be visiting friends in the Fulham Road beforehand. I wondered if she regarded it as slumming.

I took careful stock of Casilda in the flesh as she sat curled on the broad, comfortable sofa. She was wearing a dark plum hopsack suit, smartly cut, with a velvet collar to match, a huge topaz brooch, several gold bracelets, and shoes of a simple elegance that was worth the large sum she must have paid for them. Her slender legs were surprisingly long and seemed perfectly shaped in fine nylon from the slim ankles to the crossed, rounded knees and the strong, amply curved thighs that swelled into smooth, solid hips below the narrow, neat waist and fairly wide shoulders. The bosom, which had appeared to me generously full and opulent in evening dress, now, clothed but by no means concealed by a good tailor, was distinctly less obtrusive. Certainly I did not suspect Casilda of those crafty and eminently feminine deceptions that can be guaranteed by the manufacturers to take most men in with commendable regularity; but no rule of thumb so truthfully applies to a woman's tits as that seeing is believing. She was wearing no shirt under her jacket, by the harsh decree of fashion, and I looked forward with interest to a first-hand investigation of the evidence.

While she chatted with habitual ease of this and that, I studied her face more closely than her body.

There would be time, I promised myself, for every-thing. Besides, I already knew the obvious facts of her physique: she was tall but not thin, she was supple and lithe but sturdy rather than lissome, lean or muscular. Her limbs and her whole bearing had kept the energetic, fresh appeal of youth, unspoiled but ripened with the steadier strength, the more harmonious balance of maturity. She had the poise, the power, the sleekness of a big, beautiful, tawny jungle cat, with all the cat's languor, dignity, control and grace in action. Her head, too, was catlike, for the large, widely-set eyes and the high cheek-bones seemed to fill the broad face, except for the flash of white teeth in her great red mouth when she smiled, as she frequently did. The somewhat flat features, the bronzed yellow tinge to the skin, unlined and glowing, and the slant of the eyes themselves, despite their open shape and hazel hue, gave her an exotic look that might well have been inherited from a faint, distant touch of East Indian blood. 'Javanese or not,' I thought to myself, 'they must have rolled her in saffron as a baby.'

Casilda gave me an entertaining account of the visit she had just paid to her friends, the artistic couple, in their Chelsea studio. I was not very astonished to learn that they were women, both of them – and, of course, lesbians. But their marriage, it appeared, had gone on the rocks and was cracking up fast. Summoned by distress signals, Casilda had listened with sympathy to their joint and separate tales of woe. While vainly attempting to effect a reconciliation between the bedraggled lovebirds, she found herself suddenly courted from either side. These fervent and unexpected overtures had amused her at first by their sheer absurdity, as she put it. 'I'd do almost anything to help the old monsters,' she said, 'and I'm not easily shocked – but really what a nerve! Who can they have taken me for? By now, I suppose they'll have made it up and at this very moment are busy consoling each other in a flood of remorseful tears! It's too disgusting. I hate to think what Helen would say if she knew.'

'But doesn't she?' I asked. 'Surely you don't hide anything from Helen? I should imagine that she has a terribly jealous temperament, and that you could never risk her digging up such secrets on her own.'

Casilda laughed. 'I am my own mistress,' she said. 'As well as Helen's.' She swallowed the rest of her martini, and handed me the empty glass. 'But I didn't come here to talk about myself,' she added. 'I came to get a new angle on the seamy side of a gentleman's life.'

'From one seamy side to the other?' I inquired, adding hastily: 'Sex in Fulham Road, I mean – won't that do, as a revelation, for one afternoon?'

'Oh, there was nothing new there, I'm afraid.' She sighed, with boredom rather than regret, 'Anyhow, the afternoon is over, it's evening already and I have, as you know, an insatiable appetite.'

'You will dine with me? But I would say it was a bit early still. . . .'

31

'Thank you, I can't. Helen is expecting me back to dinner. Also, my appetite is not so easily satisfied. We will go out some other night perhaps, if you'll ask me again. Right now I am holding you to your word in a different connection. You promised to tell me a story, which I'm quite sure is fascinating. Unless you made it all up on the spur of the moment to annoy Helen. In that case you got me here under false pretences. I told you that I am curious by nature. I adore to hear other people's sexual experiences. It's a hobby of mine, an obsession, and I confess to it freely. Don't please pretend that I'm shocking you. From what Helen says I supposed that you were unshockable. Like me. Everyone assures me – my men friends included – that I have an entirely masculine outlook on such matters – meaning Sex with a big snaky capital S. Maybe they are right, at that. I can't have enough of the subject – in conversation at least. Most dirty stories leave me cold, mind you – if they're not extremely witty, they're just wishful thinking, like masturbation. No adult person should stoop to self-abuse, in my opinion. I'm sure you agree. But a true story can be shared. It imparts a genuine emotion. Whether you know the people involved or not makes no difference. Eavesdropping has its own special charm – and I personally get immense pleasure, a particular kick, as an onlooker. Either figuratively or literally, give me a ringside seat and I'll be happy. More than happy – enchanted. I would rather have Peeping Tom's role than Lady Godiva's, any day. Few women understand my attitude – and I see their point. But that is how I am made. I am counting on you to excite me with a wealth of lurid details from your past. You are the first intelligent and cultured rapist I ever met. They are usually even more to be pitied than their wretched victims, I imagine. Probably you, on the contrary, are to be envied. You're practically a professional seducer, they tell me – or have warned me. But that's nothing. Because, as we all know, two can play at the game. It takes two to play it properly, in fact. There is only one thing that you can do, as a man, that I cannot. Other sensations I, as a woman, am allowed by nature to share, to enjoy in my own way, or even, with artificial aids, to imitate. Forgive me for being so frank, I may entice a man, and use him, if I will, to a greater advantage than he could ever guess. And yet I cannot claim to have him without his having me. I must grant him the chance to boast – or at any rate to gloat on the idea – of taking, of possessing me, however briefly or incompetently or indecisively. My sole recourse, my one prerogative is to deny him that chance by rejecting his advances and withholding my favours – which is often nothing better than form of cutting off my nose to spite his face. Not that I would change my sex – Lord forbid! I'm delighted to be a woman, and ask for no more of life than contentment in the female condition. Ours is the richer part. But rape – the actual, physical forcing of oneself upon another human being, without her consent or desire, with no need for cajoling, persuasion or surrender, merely by the instinct of lust for its own sake – that is an act which I can only imagine. And the masculine side of my mentality relishes the thought of it, I am bound to admit.'

There was a pause. Then she said: 'After that long speech, I'm dying for another martini.'

I walked across the room and busied myself with the shaker. Meanwhile I embarked upon the tale that she wished to hear. A few moments before, I had been firmly resolved not to let her wheedle one word out of me: I was embarrassed, I refuse to be bullied or patronised, and – damn it – why should she always get things her own way? I wondered, as I talked, whether crass middle-aged vanity had not clouded my fitting tactical sense of this peculiar situation – but I believe the simple truth was that her frankness disarmed me. I had never met a woman who spoke and thought in this fashion. There was no doubt that she was a freak – an engaging, beguiling freak, a sort of hermaphrodite, combining the magnetic appeal of a gloriously feminine anatomy with the admirable, essentially male qualities of candour, intelligence, companionship and plain sensuality. Her direct approach to sex, led and governed by an inquiring emotion and sentiment captivated me, filling my nostrils with the bright, sharp tang of an early morning landscape, newly hosed streets, or a breeze off the sea. Her calm, clear voice swept away the shabby garbage, the mounds of conventional refuse that clog the corridors linking impulse to idea, instinct to action, body to brain. She was a strange creature, but a creature after my own heart.

Casilda leaned back against the cushions, a faint smile playing about the corners of her mouth. As I finished my story, sparing no details, she finished her drink to the last drop. I fetched her another.

'That's very kind of you,' she said. 'A perfect host. You mix excellent martinis and tell an enthralling story, with equal skill. Excuse me, won't you, if I don't blush for shame? Both the potions – alcoholic and pornographic – elated me, though I suppose I ought to rebuke you, on behalf of your sex, for your treatment of that poor, defenceless girl. Still, she probably enjoyed it in spite of herself, if we only knew. But you were a cad not to make any amends or send her some form of reward.'

'She sued the company and got damages out of them, I gather. No bastard offspring was the result on that occasion. I am not so deeply sorry for my crime. It is a woman's privilege, of course, that she can conceal her pleasure in the act, whereas no man can hope to fool his partner on that score. His orgasm is a secret that will out. All the same I got the definite impression that Miss Morley felt herself not wholly unrequited for her pains.'

'Perhaps not,' mused Casilda. 'The incident might have started a lasting friendship. I would love to have seen her face throughout the performance, from the rise to the fall of the curtain.'

'Her tail end, I assure you, was far prettier – and, I bet, no less expressive.'

Casilda gave me her gay, light, bubbling laugh, pulled on a glove, and sat up straight, as if to go.

'You baffle me,' I remarked. 'I simply cannot picture you as a lesbian. It's not convincing. You have so few hallmarks. Yet you remain faithful to Helen. You rush back to her whenever she calls or expects you. How long has that affair been going on?'

Casilda relaxed with a slight shrug of her shoulders, and examined her pink-gloved fingertips with care.

'Oh,' she answered, and was silent. 'Well . . . it's a matter of habit – an agreeable one, and no trouble. I'm devoted to Helen. She has been kind, and she is sweet. I won't pretend that I don't love her – and I like what we do together. I dote on being adored. But you're wrong to imagine I'm faithful to her. Far from it. She forgives me my lapses, poor darling – when she catches me out. She has to. So I try to deceive her on the quiet – because she can't exist without me, or not for long, and jealousy sickens her. It makes her ill. But in this whole thing the passion – or no, the emotion – is a little one-sided, really. She doesn't see that. She will never understand me – not if it lasts forever. But I don't mind. No, I'm not homosexual. Most certainly I am not. I would hate to miss so much . . . it is just that I would as soon go to bed with a woman as a man. Sometimes. Not always – but as often as not. Women's bodies attract me more, usually – and satisfy me less. There are different degrees, different kinds of desire for us. A man may arouse them all; and a woman can't – that's the sad part of it – though I may want her as much, and often her need for me is twice as intense as male lust, so I find it harder to reject or resist; it flatters me more. Still, there is no valid comparison – if you like, it's rather the same as wines and spirits. I prefer a good wine. I can drink any quantity I am offered; but I need my hard liquour too, from time to time, like everyone else – unless I happen to have gone on the wagon, as I do occasionally. Helen is my staple vintage, for regular consumption – not as regular as she could wish, I'm afraid. I would hesitate to call her a *vin ordinaire*, though. She's superb in bed. I'd be a fool to give her up.'

'Both of you were unhappily married when you took to each other,' I insinuated.

'Maybe,' Casilda replied. 'She's much nearer to being a true lez than I am. The instinct was there, deeply buried, long before Lucien began to neglect her – which he very soon did, almost completely. But she didn't seduce me. I mean, it wasn't the first time in my case – though it was in hers. Helen's a terribly moral person, according to her lights. She has rigidly strict principles, and insists on living up to them. I had the devil of a time getting her to make love to me, although she was in love with me, desperately, and had been for years. Neither of us has ever regretted it since, I don't think – but that is perhaps the main reason for my tremendous hold on her: I led her astray. She is the lover mostly, and I am the loved – but it is I who am the wicked one, in her view of things. She won't let me forget it. Still, what do I care? It salves her conscience – and there is nothing worse than a conscience in bed, don't you find?'

I nodded. 'When did you discover that?'

'Oh, I've always known it. I'm a healthy girl, I hate hypocrisy – or any other trumped-up complication. It was like that with me from the very start. I took Helen in my stride, you might say.' She smiled. 'She came a good way down the list. I had seduced myself, to all intents, as a schoolgirl, right at the beginning. With the games mistress. So, you see, I couldn't be more normal. It was the classic gambit.'

'What age were you?'

'Oh, I was a senior. A prefect. Rising sixteen.'

'And a virgin?'

'Yes – that all happened at about the same time. A couple of weeks later, in the holidays. It seems a century ago. I'm over twenty-seven. My romp with the games mistress was fine and dandy in its way, as an eye-opener – but it left me in an even more inquisitive mood than before. I am horribly inquisitive by nature, as you know – and always was. I made a ghastly mistake – which is also quite normal, I gather.'

'You mean you were let down, and that is why you prefer your own sex to mine?'

'I've told you I don't, *au fond*. It didn't put me off men for long. But I chose badly – as I guessed, or half-realised, at the time. He was much more of a virgin than I was, though he struck me then as wonderfully grown-up, almost old. A boy of about twenty-two. The clumsy lout! God knows I made it easy enough for him. But he hurt me like hell. In a punt one night on the river at Cambridge. I must have screamed like a stuck pig. It was shameful, messy and revolting. How I bled, and how I loathed him! The brute – he didn't even do the job properly. I found that out afterwards, though for the moment I felt sure he had killed me. In my next incarnation I shall plump for the bank. Never deflower a girl in a punt, Tony.'

'Very good, I'll remember your advice,' I said. 'It explains your profound fellow-feeling for Miss Morley.'

'Ah no, that was done without her consent. I've never been raped in that sense. Sometimes it has been rather the other way about; there's a certain added zest for me in a quick, animal encounter of that kind with a total stranger. It's the masculine side of me again, I suppose, that grabs what it wants, with no questions asked, no strings attached, and no preliminaries. They're so often a bore – all those tiresome *hors d'oeuvres* – if one's just hungry and in a hurry for a snack . . . I'll never buy myself a gigolo if I live to be ninety. But a hither look and your latchkey will work the trick as neatly as a dive into the nearest thicket for cover. I'm considered good-looking, I know, but it seldom presents any difficulty to get oneself laid – even for the Miss Morleys of this world – if that's what one is after. They take you for a cheap whore, not unreasonably – and treat you as such. That is partly the attraction for me. But because you're a free gift they won't turn rough on you – not too rough. I picked up a gorgeous Swede in a hotel lift once – just took him by the hand and led him to my room. I believe that's the common practice in Sweden – whereas a man followed me in Harrods the other day, so I pushed the stuttering idiot ahead of me into a taxi and we drove to his flat in Kew for a tumble. I remember similar incidents occurring more or less on the dance floor, on a park bench in Italy during my second honeymoon, and against some very hard and grimy railings in the blackout. But who doesn't? Helen, for one, of course. No – maybe I'm wrong, at that. Most girls wait to be introduced to a man before he can touch them. But there are some men I want that I don't want to see again. I'm glad to save them the bother. Frequently, then, they pester you to tell them your name. I still keep the cards of two gentlemen who expected me to follow up what was indeed a pleasant if passing introduction. One of them I often see around in the West End, he is always trying to get to meet me socially. I sold myself to him for ten minutes – at a whacking high price – in an upstairs room over a restaurant. He's a stockbroker. It was a flag day. Fearfully hot. I gave him all the flags I had left, for fifty pounds. At least he swore that he got his money's worth, after accusing me of scandalous dumping. But the fleeting adventure I most enjoyed at the time was a whale of a set-to I had with a Mexican – Lieutenant-General Arcadio Jesus Maria Quintana Zunzunegui, on his card – in a crowded compartment all one night on the train journey across France from Lausanne. He began it as soon as I settled behind my newspaper and magazines in the seat facing his. He put a rug over my knees and a well-manicured hand between them. We were by the window, but there were six other passengers packed in with us. It was agonisingly difficult not to squirm, and almost as hard not to laugh. He leaned far forward from the edge of his seat and never took his eyes off the cover of the *Vogue* I pretended to be reading. He was a funny little fellow, but absolutely indefatigable. I didn't get a single wink of sleep; he never let up for a moment. I could not make him stop, and it would have been too risky to move the rug and try to escape into the corridor. His caresses were incredibly artful. He was adept at delaying and prolonging the most exquisite sensations in me to the sheerest brink of ecstasy. I bit my lips till they bled. I was literally crying for mercy – for some final respite, either way. It wasn't that I couldn't reach the climax – I did, again and again. But it was never quite over, it went on still, the whole time . . . if only I could have come! But coming I was, continually, without a pause, except for infinite variations in the degree of my torment and delight. Whenever I got to the very end of my tether and was almost on the point of screaming, when I could bear it not another instant, this diabolical Mexican would withdraw his hands for a while, to stroke my thighs or tickle my short hairs and gently pinch my belly. I was young, not yet seventeen, though I

41

looked older. I was terrified, too, that we were being watched. That may have been the cause of it. But I have never had the same sensations since, I promise you.'

'What happened in the end?'

'I scrambled out into the passage, and lurched along to the lavatory. It was no good: he followed close on my heels, opened the door for me – and shut it behind us.'

'Didn't anybody see you?'

'There was no one about – that time. But he led me back there again in the morning and two people were waiting in line by the door when we came out. It was awful.'

'And possibly a bit cramped inside?'

'Yes – but we didn't even notice. It was over in a flash, as you can imagine.'

'How?'

'He sat down and pulled me on to his – er – lap. I must say the General was magnificently armed.'

'Which way did you face?'

'Towards each other, as we had been in the compartment. I straddled him, on the first occasion. The next time, just before daybreak, he spun me around and skewered me from the rear. It took slightly longer. I think the men outside must have heard us. Not a word had passed between us until then. I still didn't speak – but he poured out a whole flood of endearments, and I expect I contributed a fair amount to the din.'

'You have a deliciously vivid memory. I admire you for that. It's marvellous. Vicarious pleasures are almost all that's left to me, at my advanced age. Like you, I revel in sex even at second or third hand. I could listen to such tales for hours at a stretch. No, no, don't go – for heaven's sake! Let me fix you a drink. I'm fascinated. Tell me, how on earth did you get rid of him?'

'Eventually I shook him off in Paris. I was determined to keep my distance – which didn't make sense to him. He was going home to run a revolution, and implored me to string along with him and see it through. I like prying and spying into the sexual habits of my fellow men and women, especially if they are the friends of my most intimate friends – or complete strangers. But nine times out of ten I don't, myself, wish to become involved. Mine isn't the typically feminine kind of curiosity. I may have their shamelessness, but women, I've found, are only drawn to sex for love of the emotion they can get or give with the body. A man, though more selfish, more importunate, far more clumsy and eager, is generally not so personal, so limited, so romantic. Of course he doesn't live for sex, as we do; he just wants it handy. His attitude to the business may be scientific, literary or merely biological. Yet men don't like a girl to look on sex in the same way as they do. You have to enjoy it for their sakes, not as a vital private experience on its own. Your interest in sex is something that they demand from you as an exclusive gift, a sort of fulfilment of their personality. They say they want you to share it with them – but it has got to be all theirs, when you get down to it.'

'That's only natural, while they're in love with you.'

'I don't agree. Look – my second husband was an Englishman, but not of the common-or-garden variety. He taught me a great deal. I cannot think of any caress, any method of love, that he did not practise to perfection and lavish on me. I needn't go into details, or even you would consider the story long-winded. He brought tarts to the house, he urged pals of his to make passes at me, he stripped me naked and fondled me in these chaps' presence, he used ropes, gadgets and fetishes galore, there was nothing he would not do in front of me or induce me to play at for his amusement. I didn't object. Most of his whims were peculiar but highly exciting. I'm not one to hang back at any invitation, however novel or laborious. But the fellow, frankly, was depraved. He was downright degenerate. I left him after a few months of incessant orgies. Do you know why? Because he hated me to enjoy any part of it. For a time I made a pretence of being cold, horrified, nauseated. That was what he wanted – once we were married. Until then he had seemed normal. An ingenious, exhausting, unquenchable lecher, who vented his ruttish passion on me a dozen times a day – but I could take it. His enthusiasm flattered me at first, then it frightened me; finally I was disgusted. He was Priapus, and all his extravagant lunacies were devised to prove it to me, for his own joy and glory.'

'Well?' Casilda had fallen silent, frowning over her cocktail.

'We went on our honeymoon to the South of France. Motoring back, we stayed at a quiet country hotel. And he was shocked – imagine! – violently shocked and furiously angry, because I listened, with my ear pressed against a thin partition, to the couple next door. They were probably on their honeymoon also. We had seen them that evening at dinner. He was an earnest, nondescript young man, who wore glasses. She was rather sweet – in a well-brought-up way, pale, pretty, and unpainted. But, my word, how they shagged, those two! I didn't hear him at first, or guess it was her. I thought someone was sick, mortally sick, at their last gasp. She moaned, she mumbled, she called upon her Maker, panting, letting out sudden shrill yelps of anguish. Then I recognised a male's hoarse, strained, heavy breathing and the regular creaking crescendo of springs. I was in our bathroom, which adjoined theirs, with one wall evidently running alongside the bed itself. From the way she carried on, really he might have been throttling her! Such a little innocent to look at, but she had taken to the game like any ugly duckling to water. I listened . . . by stopping up my other ear, with one cheek flat against that wall, I got every sound. I was pleasurably tired myself, mark you – not to say groggy from fornication and praying for a snatch of sleep. But this intimate symphony next door, the grunting of the two-backed beast in heat, like a human locomotive in action, was wildly exciting. I sprang up from the bidet and rushed to fetch Rupert – he ought not to miss it. I, an eavesdropper

45

of long standing, so to speak, had never heard such a grand, full-throated performance. Talk of ballet or opera! This had words, music, movement – the lot. Her monologue was neither inarticulate nor obscene enough for my taste, to tell you the truth – but I may by hypercritical. Blasphemy repels me at any time, but particularly from a woman in the throes of coition, and more so if she's a convent-bred bride unconsciously babbling her bliss in religious terms. Leave that to the man, as his right. It is *his* act of creation, after all; ours comes later. I prefer the poetry of the good dirty words; they are sublime, too. Anyway, Rupert wasn't interested. He lost his temper and shouted like a maniac, cursing me for a foul-minded slut and asking how *I* would like *my* privacy invaded by lurking, cowardly neurotics who had nothing better to do than to frig themselves with lascivious, cerebral impotence at the signs overheard of my innermost rapture. I was flabbergasted – but there was no arguing with him. I dashed back to my coign of vantage – just in time for the finale. Rupert was utterly incensed; he sulked for days afterwards. And he never forgave me. He kept throwing it in my face when his weird notions revolted me, or when I fell in with some complicated, salacious scheme of his – which was always supposed to be for our mutual enjoyment. "You love the part of the passive spectator, don't you?" he would say. "Then watch this!" Or he'd put a garish, shop-worn floozy to work on me with her mercenary, mechanical cunning and exclaim: "Now you know what fun it is to do the belly dance

46

in public." The last straw that broke our marriage was one of these frolics, when he had a reeling-drunk Irishman in tow, who was actually an old jilted suitor of mine, and tugged the brassy bitch off me as soon as she was through, so that Mick should "go ahead, my dear fellah, and finish the job properly" while he and his hireling held me down, before ordering us to "shift over there, and we'll show you how to poke." I had realised by that time what his sadistic kink was – but at this early stage in France I didn't have a clue. And it wasn't as if I had jumped from his arms and fled to the bathroom at the wrong physiological moment. On the contary, even he was satiated – but awake, not actually aching for a rest, as I was. No, he was jealous of my independence, mad with the morbid envy of inverted puritanism. Later on I learned that he had been warped in adolescence by semi-incestuous idolisation of his mother, a famous Edwardian beauty who was as naughty as they come. I was to be his ideal, as pure as the driven snow – and he would do the driving. What he craved was a fallen angel who is not common property but a private pupil, wide-eyed and pleading to be debauched in the headmaster's study. Up to a point I indulged his fancy. But he failed to break my spirit – my personal freedom, my sensual idiosyncrasies, my choice of pet vices, my detachment, which he deplored as selfishness, greed and cynicism.'

I was standing behind Casilda as she ceased talking and glanced at her watch. I bent over the sofa, lifted up her wrist, and kissed it. I peeled off the one pink glove, then ran my fingers round her neck and stroked her nape and shoulders. To do this I unbuttoned the jacket, lest I should spoil its line, while tipping her chin towards me. Her breasts remained covered under the open lapels, for they were set far apart, like a prancing chariot team linked by a frail lace halter. We gazed at each other searchingly, in silence, during those slow, timeless minutes that stir and start the blood in languid motion through the veins. Casilda closed her eyes and smiled. She, who was no enigma when she talked, seemed faintly mysterious to me now. Here we paused, lingering on this familiar threshold that is always new. Would she bid me a gentle good-night and turn away? Calmly my mind pondered on acceptance of the thought. I resolved to let her alone if she wished. Everything was changed between us, as one's whole being changes at the crucial moment when the decision is already taken, and tacitly agreed, but still may be withdrawn, before the bond is sealed. We were no longer as we had been a single sudden second ago. There was the contact, the touch on the lever, the spark that hung upon a command, to be born or denied at one quick motion, one last irrevocable gesture.

'No, Tony, not now,' Casilda murmured. 'I must leave you.'

By then it was too late. My clear intention of a flickering instant since was gone. I could not now bow to defeat. The warm, creeping tingle of desire was in my body, glowing in my loins, rousing my manhood, pulsing through me, clamouring for battle. Ah, what delirious happiness to feel again this thrilling call to action! I rejoiced in these first symptoms of a glad state which nowadays, under the threat of enforced chastity, was all too seldom vouchsafed to my waning constitution. They mustn't be neglected; I could not afford to ignore them wastefully when the raised finger of opportunity beckoned. Seizing the ripe fruit within my grasp. I plunged my clutching hands into Casilda's undefended bosom, releasing its twin splendours from their flimsy imprisonment, as I crushed my mouth on the soft, intoxicating treasure of her parted, pouting lips. Thirstily I absorbed their sweet, refreshing fire, while baring her firm breasts to receive an awaited steady shower of ardent kisses. Well might she be proud of their young arrogance, I reflected, as I weighed, fondled and tested them like a gardener or greengrocer examining his wares – holding them in my palms and lightly pinching the small nipples – the model for a luscious masterpiece which Mother Nature chose to copy in alternate versions, as the raspberry or the wild strawberry. With head thrown back and arms spread wide, Casilda arched herself in my embrace as I tore my mouth away at last and sprawled beside her, sampling her tits, devouring them, whipping their stiff, perky little points with my tongue. I pictured Helen relishing this amorous task. . . .

Tense but abandoned, Casilda stayed in that position, reclining on the prop of my encircling arms, while my other hand groped beneath her skirt, up thighs as smooth as silk, towards the warm, wet, tender gash that shrank and shut instinctively, like a sea anemone, at my approach, but then surrendered, clammy and afire with yearning for the delicate homage that my avid fingers would pay to the most sensitive and secret fibre of her anatomy. Her clitoris also was not large in size. For a big gal she was fashioned with a disproportionate neatness of detail. Her breasts, as I now knew, were not the apple, the orange or the pear, but slightly flattened and more heavily rounded, solid, firm and golden, like the grapefruit – yet her nipples and the hidden bud of her sex were small.

The response to my touch upon it was immediate. Her short, strong torso heaved and shuddered, her long legs stretched straight out, and for the first time since we kissed she made some slight, incoherent sound. It was a faint, plaintive sigh. Her breathing grew louder and faster. She tossed and turned her head from side to side. But this was nothing yet. I was going to teach our young Sappho a lesson. I started to undress her. I wanted her stripped. Naked she must be, at my mercy, and I too would shed all this decent covering that marred attempted intimacy, keeping us as dummies and strangers at arm's length. I'd show this voluptuous, misguided slut what she was missing since she took up with Helen. . . .

'No, no,' she whispered. I was trying to unfasten her skirt.

With a hand on my forehead she thrust me gently away.

'I despise making love with one's clothes on,' I complained.'

'So do I – but you won't,' she remarked with a smile. 'I mean, we aren't going to. I'm not giving in to you now. Not tonight. Ssh – be quiet! Because I say so.

As she spoke, she ran her fingers through my hair and kissed me lightly on the cheek, while the other hand darted down to a lower level and found what it was searching for. Ah, but damnation and hell, the traitor did me less than justice! She clasped my member in a fond, sure, gentle grip, as if to soothe an aching pain. A moment ago he had made his defiant presence felt against her flank, but no sooner did she greet him in this courteous manner, trotting him out into the open, than some blight of inexplicable shyness overcame him, and he appeared, hanging his swollen head with surly embarrassment and blushing deeply. It was obvious that he lacked all zeal and appetite for combat. His brief enthusiasm had quickly dwindled. What was the point of entering on such a venture at half-cock? I cursed him bitterly under my breath, and in my turn drew back sharply from Casilda's arms.

I noticed then that her face still wore a charitable smile, as if to pardon the grievous incivility of my physical indifference. There was nothing for it. All hope of gallantly displaying my male authority over her had crumpled. But she herself was not the kind

51

that gives up easily. She slipped to the floor on her knees, and studied the matter in hand at close range – with loving care and a good deal of amusement. I was powerless to stop her doing what I now saw she intended. She cupped my testicles in a softly squeezing grasp and tickled the stem of my penis, from the knob to the root, with her tongue. It was unbelievably deft, her tongue – it rang all the changes and excuted every tune of my flute, so that even that woebegone, overworked instrument could scarcely endure the ordeal. She led it a dance that began as a stately pavane and developed, through a succession of varying rhythms, from a merry hornpipe, a wild fandango and lilting waltz, into a riotous can-can and a frenzied highland fling. She rubbed it and pressed it between her lips, which were like moist, warm rose-petals drenched in sunshine and summer showers – and finally, as the night filled with stars before my eyes, she swallowed it whole. She ate me alive – and left me limp, blind and gasping, faint, trembling, weary and drained to the dregs. Never before had I known what it was to be gamohuched in this way – to the hilt of extinction, as it were. The joke was on me.

I picked myself up off the sofa when she returned, in a moment or two, from the bathroom. She blew me a kiss from the doorway.

'I must rush,' she said. 'I'm frightfully late. Helen will be as sour as mud.'

'I'm sorry. My car's out of order, but – '

'Never mind. She'll forgive me.' Casilda gave a happy, expectant chuckle of laughter in her throat.

'And it's you that she will have to thank – for putting me in such a fine frisky mood. There, think of that – you wicked man!'

'Run along now – you mustn't keep her waiting. That would be too bad. But please,' I begged, 'don't tantalise me! Don't – damn you – tantalise me!'

'Why?' She gazed at me with great big open eyes that now looked dewily innocent and blue. 'Surely you're not jealous of Helen?'

'Oh, stop it!' I cried. 'Shut up, get out! What wouldn't I give to watch, to see you both, to be there. . . .'

'Would you, now?' She laughed again. 'Then so you shall – if I can arrange it. I'll think. I'll try to find a way. Good-bye. Good night.'

The pink glove turned the handle of the door, and she was gone.

CHAPTER THREE

Once or twice in the course of the next weeks –
though we met all too seldom for my liking – I
tried to remind Casilda of her promise, which had
left me on tenterhooks of anticipation. I found her
constrained and awkward about it, however. Each
time I broached the subject she would frown, give
a short nod, and with a hasty 'Yes, yes, we'll see,'
whisk off at a tangent, like a billiard ball. It was
clear that she regretted ever having made the offer
to let me in on her amorous entanglements with
Helen. Or else she was quite stumped for a means
of bidding me to the feast without Helen's knowledge. Obviously one ruled out any chance of her
talking Helen into a threesome; the very idea was
fantastic, preposterous. For all Casilda's hold over
Helen, coax, cajole, bully or blackmail her as she
might, the mere suggestion of such indecency would

have put an abrupt and bitter end to their affair forever. Imagine profaning their sacred, sisterly love with a *man* in the room – and me of all men! But the alternative – to smuggle me into the wings somehow, or hide me under the bed as a stowaway – was almost equally difficult. I had an excellent pair of binoculars in my possession, as I told Casilda jokingly – yet, even if they had done for this purpose, at long range half the beauty of the spectacle would have been lost on me, naturally. As a voyeur, I hate to miss the sounds and the atmosphere that are complementary to the actual thrill of seeing the players in motion – especially when one cannot or must not touch, so that ultimate satisfaction, come what may, is impossible.

I did not dare to insist or appear too keen on the giddy treat that Casilda had pledged herself to provide for me, since it had begun to fade into thin air like a mirage. She had thought better of it, and my reverting to the topic would only jeopardise the cheerful affection she showed towards me on the rare occasions when we were able to meet. Far from giving any indication that her first visit *chez moi* had left an ugly taste in her mouth, the dear girl was most friendly and obliging. In a subtle way, without either reticence or obscenity, she managed to combine the best of both worlds, for she was sensitive but never sentimental, wholly uninhibited but quiet and sensible, frankly sensual, even lascivious, but neither neurotic nor depraved. Sex did not defile or cheapen her with any taint of that rabid nymphomania which compels the sufferer to seek frequent, impatient, vain relief for the aching void of her vagina. In Casilda's case the mean was truly happy.

'Flippancy or whimsy I can stand,' she confessed, 'but coyness and facetious persiflage are the devil.' I christened her Messalina Incorporated – or Sappho II, like a yacht – and my apprecation of her 'androgynous attitude to love' made her smile. She could abandon all control in the total surrender of her typical self without upsetting her mental balance in the slightest degree. Her poise bore no trace of pose. She would celebrate the sacred carnal rites of the altars of the oldest mystery with none of the pious mumbo jumbo that mars the cooperation of many an addicted and accomplished votaress in the ineffably simple frenzy of the sexual act.

Or so I believed. I could not have sworn that it was true, for lack of proof. Some unconscious restraint kept us in check. We did not choose to copulate. I had not taken Casilda, and she did not give herself to me. Looking back on that time, under two years ago, I am at a loss to explain exactly what retarded the normal development of our intimate acquaintance to its foregone conclusion. We saw each other only in secret, when Helen's social engagements permitted; there was no hope of our sleeping together in the full meaning of the phrase – but even so we had plenty of opportunities to cuckold her thoroughly and time enough, surely to 'leap into bed,' as the silly saying goes, for a hurried 'roll in the hay.'

56

I wonder still why we dallied so long on the brink. Casilda has since assured me – and she is the soul of honesty – that it was not for my sake, to spare me embarrassment, that she steadfastly refused to consummate our mutual desires, but preferred to appease them by other methods. I glumly suspected that she had assumed I must be impotent – or physically incapable of proper intercourse. The idea that she might have gained this unflattering impression from my deplorably feeble showing at our first skirmish worried me to distraction. I was determined to prove her wrong. I would vindicate myself up to the hilt at the earliest possible juncture. Yet somehow that juncture never occurred, the supreme moment never came, the situation did not arise. I grew desperately alarmed – to the point where I would have failed ingnominiously, I am convinced, if Casilda had not used the utmost tact in avoiding the issue. I suppose she realised that, caught up as I was in a welter of wounded pride, expectations, lecherous vanity and doubt, we were treading on dangerous ground. One false move on her part might bring our budding romance to instant and final catastrophe, she may have felt. Perhaps it is not surprising that she diagnosed and sought to treat me as a pathological case. I, in my anxiety, was acquiring a serious complex about the problem in possessing her – utterly at last, in complete fulfilment, without further thwarting delays. I was becoming frantically tired of this prolonged beating about the bush. Yet – almost literally – she slipped through my fingers.

Whenever I tried to clinch the argument, she employed the same evasive tactics with absolute success.

Why did I let her get away with it? Was I, at my age, a greenhorn so gullible and guileless that I must succumb to the crafty but rudimentary stratagems of any plain tart's amorous technique? Not even the most innocent duellist, in the first flush of youth, would have sat back contentedly, as I did, and allowed a slut to fob him off in such a one-sided fashion, however great might be the artistry she applied to the task or the pleasure he derived from her skilful ministrations. And yet with me the trick worked, more than once. The scene on the sofa was repeated at least a couple of times when Casilda came to call. She would spend a happy half-hour browsing among my books or pouring over my fine collection of photographs and sketches – the pick of my library. I refer, of course, not to my regular stock in trade as an art dealer but to the various shelves and portfolios crammed with erotic treasures. Of these, though I say it myself, I have many magnificent specimens, gathered and stored through the years; Casilda, as I had guessed, took a typically masculine interest in such curios. She would examine each detail, in spellbound silence, with grave and meticulous care, never biting off more than she could chew at one session, but concentrating her attention on a single set of illustrations at a time. When her curiosity was slaked – and her senses inflamed – she would beckon smilingly to me and, with an almost jaunty little sigh, exchange the lickerish images of venery in two dimensions for the tangible, stirring, more colourful reality within her grasp. She wanted to be made love to. I seized her in my arms, and caressed her from top to toe with all the mingled tenderness and vehemence of pent-up, famished passion.

I ought to have laid her then and there, pounding the anvil while the iron was hot. Something prevented me. I had no wish to rape her. The ordinary slow process of seduction by degrees was going to suffice. She must demand it, she must want to have me herself, summoned, needed, welcomed within her. Not that I belong to the effeminate breed of lover who has to be carried across the threshold like some trembling bride. But my courage deserted me. I did not even manage to strip her naked on these occasions. Always before I could snatch the last wisp of clothing from her body, to reveal the living sculpture, the statue of flesh that I was about to enter, to impale and penetrate, to strangle, invade and use as my own property by right of conquest, she would contrive to escape, eluding my embrace as swiftly and smoothly as a snake slithering away into the grass or a stately schooner casting off her moorings. She gave me no time to complain. Only sheer force would have stopped her. I had to let her have her head, after it was too late. 'No, darling,' she murmured. 'No – not just yet, not now.' That was her invariable plea, the same urgent whisper that had defeated my purpose, unmanning me, at every previous attempt. And it was all she could say for a while, because then her lips closed greedily upon the beautiful big lollipop which she was licking and tickling with her tongue, as she observed me quizzically from the point of vantage where she had now installed herself, squatting on the floor between my knees, her elbows across my thighs.

She won; she did as she liked with me. I was a fool to submit. This anteroom prologue suited her low plan; I should have ordered her through to the bed next door. She hoodwinked me disgracefully – but so enjoyably that I soon forgot my anger and indignation against her. A younger man would have rebelled at her taking matters into her own hands with such bareface aplomb. I could only chide her and protest when it was over. A cockteaser I called her.

'At heart that's all you are – just a slick little cockteaser. You're a dodger, a shirker, a cheat – a charming one, but vicious. And peculiarly unemancipated – in spite of your brave claims.'

She simply scoffed at my sour look of frustration, which may not have been very convincing.

'Why, you beast!' she retorted. 'I think you're horribly ungrateful. Didn't I do it nicely? I've been highly complimented on my special talents in that line. It's one of my specialities, I'd have you know. Gold medals and recommendations galore. In great favour with tired businessmen.'

'And pampered elderly ladies,' I added.

'Oh, there you go again! You're incorrigible.'

Sometimes we were content to behave like old

friends in each other's company: sex did not come into it. We would lunch or dine together at small restaurants where there was hardly any danger of being seen by someone we knew, or we would hide ourselves in a local cinema. She always declined to go for a drive in the country. 'No time,' she said, 'and I would rather wait until we can spend a weekend miles away, when Helen's out of town.'

It is an extraordinary admission to make – and I am loath to acknowledge the possibility – but it may be that by instinct, subconsciously, at the back of my mind I was glad not to be put to the test . . . just yet. I pretended, for appearances' sake, that I was chagrined and deeply vexed – but that was only to protect my self-esteem. Already Casilda meant far too much to me – though I would stoutly have denied her importance in my life – to run so big a risk of disappointing her. I was inwardly afraid, terribly afraid, of failure. I could not bear to envisage any outcome to our present emotional impasse short of a memorable and tremendous triumph. She must be forced to avow her ludicrous error in underrating my virility. Afterwards I might be prepared to cast her aside. I could drop her then, if I wished, like a dirty shirt. I wasn't hunting just now for a regular bedfellow, and didn't require one. But first she would have to learn in the flesh, beyond any measure of doubt, once and for all, that I was still my body's own master and able to impose its will or its whims on others.

In the circumstances the passive role of onlooker, which Casilda had dangled under my nose, was the ideal solution. I will make no bones about it, as I did at the time with her, out of some queer, involved, ambitious scruple: the very thought, the mere prospect of seeing those two in bed together was an obsession which I could not banish from my tortured brain; it stayed with me night and day, filling my dreams and every waking hour with the turbulent, crazy fancies of a forlorn hope. What a contrast they would offer, the pair of them, what a stupenduous show to watch! I could picture no spectacle, no orgy, nothing to match it. Ah, if only such a blessed bath of beauty, such a heavenly bonanza were possible! I felt I should die happy if this miracle of excitement, this private vision could be achieved – for me alone. But I knew that was too much to ask. . . .

And then one autumn evening, weeks later, it happened. I was on the point of going out to dinner with an old flame of mine and her newly-wedded husband. I had one foot in the street when the telephone's shrill semaphore lassoed me, dragging me back with an oath to answer its call. A voice spoke in tones so low and conspiratorial that at first I did not recognise Casilda on the line. 'Listen,' said the voice. 'Tony, are you there? Hold on a minute.' After a maddening pause, as I was about to hang up, my loud 'hullos' unheeded, Casilda babbled: 'Sorry. Wanted to be on the safe side . . . it's all right now. Look, I've booked you a single seat – in the front row of the stalls – for tonight. Don't get here much after eleven. Put off whatever you're doing – and come round by taxi. But only as far as the corner. . . .'

'What on earth are you talking about?' I inquired downright gruffly.

'Charity performance,' she replied. 'As You Like It – with a reduced cast of two. Sort of gala duet. Your cup of tea. I think – or so you've kept telling me for weeks, pretty well *ad nauseam.* Call beforehand, though. If anyone else answers, hang up – it'll mean the party's off. Okay?'

'Darling,' I exclaimed as the receiver clicked.

Never shall I forget the ordeal I underwent that evening, dining at Janet's. For the best part of an hour we tippled sherry while she cooked an elaborate meal. The other guests – a married couple – were in no hurry. I breathed into Janet's ear: 'I have a date, my sweet. . . .'

'Oh, I thought you were going to kiss me!' I did.

'Of course, Tony dear – but don't show off so. You always have somebody waiting for you. Still, I'll forgive you this time,' Janet agreed. 'You may be excused on important business as soon as I've served the coffee – if that's soon enough.'

I made my escape on the stroke of eleven.

'Good Heavens, Helen,' Casilda said loudly, when I got through from the nearest call-box. 'Have you forgotten your key? I'll sit up for you, to let you in. Don't be long, honey.' Then she added: 'Yes, that's all thank you, Smithers – good night,' and rang off.

Smithers, I knew, was Helen's elderly maid.

As I approached the flight of steps to the large

Regency mansion after dismissing my taxi at the entrance to the Park, the Delavignes' front door swung open, hiding Casilda, who winked at me like a schoolgirl with a finger to her lips, and silently led the way, from rug to rug, across the hall. She was wearing an ankle-length housecoat of jade-green taffeta, and once again, as she walked ahead of me, I was lost in admiration of her back view under the billowing folds that rippled and rustled darkly, like a tropic sea. The ample hips, the slender waist, the fully rounded buttocks that swayed to a rolling, majestic cadence as she sailed upstairs, their rich contours and appetising bulk presented at eye-level to my riveted gaze – this was the rear prospect that had first appeared to me on that night in September when the sight of Casilda's bottom, sheathed in clinging silk, aroused my sudden lust with a shock as swift and cruel as the lash of a whip.

Just as it was from behind that I fell for Casilda then, so now the magnetic attraction of these plump, protruding nates sent such a violent tremor tingling through my veins that I was dizzily tempted to renounce the great adventure on which we were embarked and immediately lay rough hands on this almost sitting bird that was so obviously worth two in the bush. I had a damned good mind to fling the girl face down across the nearest bed – or anywhere, on the landing if need be – and settle our old debt at once, right away, without more ado, before Helen got home.

I cannot say whether Casilda's sharp wits told

her what was brewing in her wake, but she effectively balked my barnyard intentions by hissing a rigamarole of advice to me over her shoulder as we crossed Helen's room into hers.

'Be frightfully careful, darling – don't make a sound,' she implored. 'It's Wagstaff's night out – but he'll use the back door. Smithers and Cook are asleep at the top of the house. Lucien has gone to Scotland. Anyhow, I expect you've had lots of practice in creeping about on boudoir manoeuvres of this sort. You can hide in my clothes closet meanwhile – until Helen gets in. She'll be back any minute. I shall leave our door open – though she's sure to shut it. If she does, step out on to the balcony, and sneak along there, through her window. Look – it's quite safe. The next one is Lucien's – that's your line of retreat, downstairs and straight ahead . . . I greased all the hinges myself.'

She guided me around on a rapid reconnaissance and pressed a wee pencil torch into my hand. It was a cloudy night, not raining or actually cold. The balcony overlooked a strip of gloomy garden behind the house. The stage within was nicely set: it might have been devised especially for some intricate bedroom farce. Casilda threw her arms about my neck and kissed me gaily. 'Be good,' she enjoined again in earnest. 'And you won't hate me, will you, whatever you do?'

I laughed. 'Whatever *I* do?' I asked. 'That's hardly the question. It's to be all your doing, I trust, from now on – or mostly. I shall stay quieter

65

than a mouse in the panelling, so long as you do your stuff. But I warn you I'll roar like a lion if I find you're a fake.'

'Cas-seeel-dah!' Helen's yodel echoed up from the hall – refined but imperious, and alarmingly close. We had not heard her arrive.

Her protegée pushed me into a tunnel festooned with soft, scented frocks and furs, like lianas smothering a jungle trail, and dashed away to greet Milady Delavigne, the distinguished madame of this high-class house. For what seemed eternity I remained cooped there, condemned to languish in a dark, all too fragrant padded cell, while they presumably lingered, chatting over a nightcap below. . . . Emboldened finally by boredom, I peeped out from my cubby-hole. The coast was clear. I slunk on to the balcony. There was a faint glimmer of light showing downstairs, but it was switched off after a moment, while I waited, leaning back against the wall, and then it came on behind me, shining through the thick curtains, as both their voices in animated dialogue entered the room. Casilda's, pitched loud and distinctly, approached the window saying: 'Oh yes, Cyril would, of course, he's such an idiot . . . but you must be dog-tired, my poppet. I'll see if we're getting any air in here – isn't it a leetle bit stuffy? Tell me more about that arrant hussy Flo. . . .'

Gliding through the heavily draped curtains like a ghost – a warm, benevolent ghost – she signalled me in by the French window, which she left slightly ajar at my back as she sat down on a convenient

leather pouf in the ample recess, a veritable stage
box, and was gone with a parting pat on the cheek.
There was nothing to see straight in front, through
a chink the width of a razor's edge, except the
huge, high-canopied, empty nuptial couch – but by
squinting sideways round the rim of the curtains to
the far end of the room I espied Helen at her
dressing table, swathed in a shimmering white satin
gown, with Casilda lolling in a tall chair beyond,
brandy balloon aswirl in one hand, neck comfortably propped, eyelids lowered. Helen was busy
transferring a tidy fortune from her person to a
jewel casket the size of a pirate's chest. She stood
up, and her friend helped to extract the neat, slim,
marvellous torso from its costly covers, as Helen
wriggled free, like a mermaid shedding her fishtail,
to become a pocket Venus risen from the foam, an
alabaster nymph springing to life from the pedestal
of discarded trappings coiled about her ankles.
With leisurely deliberation for my benefit, Casilda
fetched the diaphanous negligee that was chastely
to envelope the perfect proportions of an exquisite
small figure clad incongruously in skintight nylon
briefs and a strapless bra. To my sincere amazement the vision, while it lasted, was of breathtaking
purity. Helen was – how old was she? Forty-four?
Forty-two, if a day. But she was not, as I had
imagined her, remarkably well preserved for her
age: she was lovely in her own right, a priceless
Tanagra statuette, delicate, dainty, at first glance
almost girlish, and yet ideally formed, on shapely
classic lines, with every curve and facet of the trunk

and limbs impeccably drawn, trimly contrived, firmly, admirably modelled. It was a miniature, fashioned on a tiny scale, but certainly not starved or skimped in any detail, nor distressingly fragile or puny. Nothing indeed was lacking to lend all natural enchantment to this delicious little body, save only the sheer, inimitable bloom of youth itself. Charm it had, and harmony . . . but sexual energy, stamina, strength?

Helen, who had retired to the bathroom, belonged by rights in a museum. Although no doubt we would shortly see this pale porcelain shepherdess converted, under Casilda's tender care, into a raving maenad, I could scarcely conceive of her as a creature of flesh and blood, or recognise the haughty hostess whom I knew, loaded with diamonds. The transformation in any event should be worth witnessing.

Casilda was too efficient, a producer to let the attention of her audience flag in Helen's absence. She took advantage of this interval to display herself before me, stark and entirely naked at last. Floating into focus with the mannequin's slinky, calculated grace, very slowly she disrobed in a comical parody of a striptease act, divesting herself in one continuous movement of the long green wrap, a gossamer slip, a black lace brassiere, and transparent frilly panties to match. As though unleashed, rather than merely relieved of her clothes, she glided airily, imperviously, without a stitch on, to lay these flimsy trifles over a settee, and returned to face in my direction across the bed's broad, low expanse, that well-sprung wrestling ring, which cut her off at the shins. As languidly as a cat, she stretched, arching her back and raising her ribs in a voluptuous gesture that lifted the fine pectoral muscles, the gleaming, provocative swell of her breasts, which she cupped in both hands and squeezed; before pressing her palms against her haunches, belly and flanks, like some immoral masseuse. Then she drained the rest of her brandy and subsided onto the quilt, not under it, to lie there encamped, her long legs crossed, wearing a surreptitious smile, relaxed but expectant.

Helen played the opening scene as prettily as if she were an actress out to woo recalcitrant critics. She could not know that she had already melted my initial indifference. Mute and motionless for a while she hovered at the foot of the bed, absorbed in pensive contemplation of a family vista – the sunny hills and shadowed dales of a beloved anatomy, which she surveyed with the same fond longing as the traveller, homeward bound, who scours the horizon for a glimpse of his native land. When Casilda sat up to offer her the happy haven of her outheld arms, Helen responded only with a grave, mysterious nod of rapt appraisal. Thereafter the tempo changed, gradually gathering speed, increasing in fervour, rising and falling, recovering by imperceptible degrees to gain fresh impetus, drifting, dwindling into the distance but always ready to revive and renew its dominant themes in a succession of varied movements like a symphony.

I in my corner drank them in, one after the other. Enthralled, breathless, carried away, I watched the drama unfold its destined course of action, quivering with excitement, gasping and panting no less loudly, I feel sure, than the lovers themselves as they strained and yearned and struggled on the soft, spotlit stage under my staring eyes that were glued to the resplendent nudity of their flailing limbs and troubled, tense, bliss-ridden bodies. I confess that the swift, intoxicating, endless sequence of events dazzled and confused me, as sometimes at the theatre there is too much to observe and retain in one's glutted, grasping memory, which jumbles up a flood of vivid fragments in the wrong order. I remember how the play began, I recall every fleeting incident and episode, I can recapture each ravishing impression with precise clarity – but if I try to string these loose bright leads together, it is just a tiresome, doleful waste of effort.

The curtain went up when Helen's filmy garment came off. Casilda deftly removed it as Helen sank onto the bed beside her and nestled in the bosom which leaned out above her, as she snuggled under the lofty throat and tilted chin, like the jutting, painted bubs on the figurehead of a full-rigged vessel. Gently they rocked, clutched tightly in an almost maternal embrace, until Helen's featherweight prevailed and she bore her opponent down, willingly overwhelmed, her shoulders square against the sheets. Helen's small, hungry mouth had fastened upon the summit of a generous tit, which she clasped firmly in one hand, while the other roamed over all the wide, smooth surfaces of Casilda's body and probed its every crease and hollow. Sprawling with a glad air of lassitude beneath this onslaught, while Helen crouched across her stomach like a sleek black panther, Casilda lay supine yet alert in the idleness of temporary surrender, a country defeated but unbowed under occupation. In time, however, as her flesh was stirred, she started to twitch and squirm a little, until at last, her resistance sapped, she turned an expressive face towards me that I might read on its contorted features an eloquent record of Helen's work in progress. I was thankful for this kindly gesture, and with good cause, for round by round thereafter, through each successive phase of their ding-dong combat, Casilda exerted considerable ingenuity to show herself and Helen to me, if not always in the most dignified or flattering light, at least from every possible angle and to the onlooker's best advantage. It was an exhibition match, and evidently, she wanted me to get my money's worth. I did in fact receive my fill of her friend's charms, as well as all her own finer points, and no mistake. When Helen's lips skimmed her belly, when her fingers combed the curly clump of fern adorning the lush Olympian mount of no-man's-land, which is no woman's either, nor anyone's private property, since it is the universal seat of love and belongs, to its name implies, solely to Venus; when Helen's eager snout went burrowing between her thighs and nuzzled the shy

71

rose that blooms there only at a lover's touch, Casilda slewed around on the bed, lifting Helen by the hips and setting them up, as it were on an easel, for me to scan, so that I should miss no aspect of what we both regarded – fixedly – as the most entrancing view in all the world. Like the lady of the house arranging the flowers for a party, Casilda opened the bouquet presented to her by her devoted admirer as soon as the donor's back was turned. She studied, patted and stroked each precious bud and petal, displaying the whole sweet cluster of blossom as a garden of delights centred on a diminutive patch of dewy moss.

A picture of neatness it was, to be sure, Helen's quaint, cute little quim: deep, raw, red gash and all, amidst the raven's nest of her luxuriant short hairs, one felt it ought to be filled by anything but envy of even its choicest rivals. It was so smart and tidy a job as the owner herself. Casilda certainly was unable to resist the temptation of biting into this ripe black fig, so succulently split and set there between the milk-white nates as on a luscious dish of clotted cream, asking to be devoured. Casilda's chestnut mane obscured my sight. All I could see now was Helen's butting, upturned romp that leapt and bounced like a bucking bronco endeavouring vainly with wild gyrations to dislodge the stubborn rider from her tail. The effect was as droll as the antics of a tethered goat exasperated by a swarm of wasps. She could bear it no more – and I beheld her parts again, fully exposed, when she broke away suddenly and swung right about, like the mad mare she was, rearing up and hurling herself into position against Casilda's groin, which she heaved into cunning, interlocked contact with her crotch, so that their juicy, drooling slits were grafted, crushed, jammed together as though they sought by this ravenous kiss to soothe and close a single gaping wound. Hers Helen held open while she twisted and strove to entwine their lower limbs, drawing one of the other's supple legs around her waist to tie a sort of profligate lovers' knot which should seal their nether lips and join their tiny tongues, dissolving all their pain in the hot, salt taste of that one mingled mouth's saliva.

How long they continued to grapple and clash, slipping and weaving and sparring like a couple of boxers, I cannot say. It was a futile equation of minus quantities which, however well matched, could only exacerbate but never finally quench their lesbian lust that crumbled and clicked like fiery coals sputtering in the grate for want of a poker. But it rubbed me up the right way, this lurid scene of friction, I have to admit. I could barely contain myself in my hiding place behind the curtains. I held my breath, for fear of betraying my presence in the offing – and that was not all, to tell the truth, that I had to take a strong grip on, though I am no more an onanist at heart than Casilda is genuinely homosexual. Yet I did not really masturbate; it was they, the pair of them, who abused me by their shameless, pernicious example. I would instantly have extended my unsolicited compliments and most assiduous service to either of these poor fornicating females – or both, if I had been given the chance.

The naked contrast between them was as divine as I had supposed; but what I could not have guessed was that Helen's body would please me more, to some extent, than Casilda's. Even allowing for the joyous shock of its discovery a moment ago, strictly speaking, as a nude, it enchanted and fascinated me still more profoundly by reason of its pure artistic values – which were superlative – than its opposite number, which I already knew. Casilda's physique was brimful of sexual attraction; Helen's was somehow more seductive, not so exciting but – that was the word – more enticing. It was the wonderful symmetry of her shape, first of all, and then that particular quality of a radiant, fastidious elegance about her whole person that I found so moving. The frailty of this prim China doll, belied by an adorable, pneumatic bottom, the definite, impertinent, pretty little tits, even that ugly thing, her twat – a livid pink parting in the glossy mesh of jet-black pubic hair – was at once so absurd and so fetching as to kindle and captivate one's incredulous interest. Perhaps, if you searched for faults, carping exception might be taken to the big brown aureoles that seemed to smear too large a dub of cinnamon around the twin cherries topping the bosom's glistening goblets of ice cream. Ah, but how jauntily they danced, above the narrow hips as she bestrode the rolling roads of pleasure! She had a nearly grown-up daughter, I reflected. What must the child be like, compared to a mother whose beauty in middle age was such a paragon, a source of such frank astonishment to the most exacting student of feminine form? Here these two specimens were striking enough in partnership – the tall, fair girl with the glowing golden skin, the long lean curves, the tawny tuft, the solid build, and, lording it over her, the slight small dark older woman, carved out of ivory, polished, delicate and hard, a pagan goddess, a camellia, a fairy queen, and yet ... Casilda's abject slave. The sweetness of the honeycomb had dizzied, vanquished, overcome the bee.

But it was a linked sweetness infinitely sustained, as the romantic poet wrote and the dreams of my waking memory confirm. I recollect a host of sights and sounds, a plethora of visions in so short a space of time. ... I see Casilda crucified, her gritted teeth bared and choking back a noiseless scream as Helen's voracious maw sucks out, her innards. I see her fingers clutch a crumpled pillow, or hooked in Helen's hair, tugging the harpy's drowned, dishevelled head into her throbbing fork, thrusting her pelvis in an acrobatic arc against those thirsty lips, that darting adder's tongue, which will not release its lacerated prey until the fainting victim has reached her stormy climax twice. ... I see Casilda's quick recovery and prompt, pitiless revenge. Now it is Helen's turn to whimper and cry out, blurting the lovesick vows, the rasped commands that interrupt the murmurous monotone of goading, gloating exhortation, ecstasy, delirium, gratitude – all things utterable – as though she were plotting aloud the soaring graph of frantic folly, from the first flicker of libidinous instinct to the last blind paroxysm that is in solemn truth the seventh heaven. . . .

The dim grey light of a November dawn, invisible as yet, but imminent, was at my heels when I, at home, like Helen and her love, clasped in each other's arms, a hundred streets away dropped off into exhausted sleep.

CHAPTER FOUR

Three months, I thought to myself, upon my soul, that's just about enough. Everything comes to him who waits – but I damn well wasn't going to wait for Casilda much longer. It would have to be now, at once or never, I decided, and if she could not bring herself to sleep with me after all this time, then to hell with her; we had better part. I had been far too mild and patient; her shilly-shallying would have to stop, or else I'd send her packing, and not mince my words, either – that would be that. If she thought there could be any more of this tomfoolery, I'd show her how wrong she was. The worm would turn – and really I would be quite happy to see the end of Miss Vandersluys, I had begun to think.

Actually, I was waiting for her at that moment, in a Mayfair bar – an unusual place for us to meet, and not one of my most favourite haunts at the best of times. She was late. I had been pole-sitting on a high stool, drowning my sorrows – or mulling over my bitter grievance against her – for the past half hour. But she was looking even gloomier than I when finally, with a frowning absence of the slightest apology, she turned up and ordered herself a gimlet. So far as I can remember, this was our fourth rendezvous in over three weeks since Casilda had staged her special charades for me that night at Helen's.

'What's the matter?' I inquired. 'You appear extremely aggrieved or depressed.'

'I am both,' she replied in a low, angry tone. 'But who cares? It's my own fault. I've just lost myself a job.'

'Oh?'

'Yes, and I'm through with women. Horrid, vicious, gnat-brained strumpets – ugh, they're worse than men! Even more of a nuisance. . . .'

'Why? What's happened? Don't tell me you've turned over a new leaf! Has Helen been making jealous scenes? Did she catch you out once too often? Or is she deceiving you now, for a change? Perhaps I'm at the bottom of it – does she know about us?'

Casilda glowered at me in disgruntled silence. 'Don't you be an idiot, too,' she said. 'I couldn't bear it.'

'I keep asking you to explain what the trouble is,' I suggested sympathetically.

'Oh, it's only that boring Social Editress of *Chic*

. . . they're a fine magazine to work for, they pay well . . . I was afraid of this, I could see it coming. She was always half on the point of pawing me – you know what I mean. She asked me at every turn to model lingeries – 'just slip these on, darling, you'd look lovely in 'em' – as though she, and not Mrs Knoblaugh, had charge of fashion. She wanted me to pose – in the raw, of course – for a photographer pal of hers, such a talented chap, who is absolutely on the verge of becoming famous. Whenever I went to see old Knobbly she'd waylay me with a cup of tea, theatre tickets, the present of some cute little trifle that would match my eyes or go so nicely with what I was wearing. She was dying to help me, my dear, she has heaps of influence. It's true, too – especially on the paper. Now she'll do me all the dirt she can. I expect. I've lost my *Chic*, you can bet your life on that.'

'Hm, rather a pity. Couldn't you have choked her off without hurting her feelings?'

'I had kept her at arm's length up to now. All innocence I was, I smiled like an imbecile. She has never dared pop the question, I looked too horribly sweet and dumb. But today it was different. Blast the bitch – she'd been out to some very grand, important luncheon, and tottered back to the office as tiddly as an owl. There was no holding her. I didn't stand a chance. If I weren't a hefty girl, with a good right hook, I would never have got away with it . . . practically unscathed.'

'Rough stuff on those plush premises – the incident has a certain novelty value at least.'

'Rough! You should have seen the pass she made at me – and the cut I gave her over one eye. Naturally I cleaned her up a bit before I left – there was blood dripping onto the carpet – but we didn't part friends, even so. She had sobered up slightly by then, but she was still rather groggy – and starting to go all maudlin with remorse. A dreadful mess.'

Casilda ruminated glumly for long enough to swallow three gins in a row, like nips of medicine.

'Pretty funny it was, really, I guess,' she conceded with a wan smile. 'the silly nitwit tried to rape me. There was a lot of sentimental talk at first about natural attraction, and how she always had this devastating thing for me. Then she grabbed and kissed me, full on the mouth, in her own office! I was so taken aback – literally, I mean – that I fell with a thump on the desk and sat there on her blotting-pad, gaping at her blankly. Damn me, though, if her hands weren't up my skirts in a flash! She huddled down to it in her swivel-chair, frigging me for all she was worth. As happy as a sandgirl, what's more, with an ear pressed hard against my tummy, as if auscultating that area to note my reaction.'

'Didn't you stop her.'

'My sweet, how could I? I was laughing too much inside – and maybe the gurgling in my guts encouraged her. But it was utterly crazy. Her secretary might have pranced in any minute – or one of that bunch of pansies who flourish on *Chic*.'

'They'd have knocked, surely?'

'Yes, but only to sweep straight ahead without pausing for a second. She wouldn't even have lifted her nose from the grindstone. She was past caring. And anyway I was powerless. She had got me pinned on the edge of the desk, with an arm round each of my legs, from underneath, holding them apart and me fixed in place, astride her lap, leaning back on my elbows . . . watching the door. This is how she had me.' Casilda swung backwards on the barstool, in a discreet demonstration of a defenceless, semirecumbent position.

'I see,' said I, reflectively. 'So that was how she had you.'

'What do you mean? Well, almost.' Casilda laughed.

'Only I picked up this great big expensive silver cigarette box, when things began to get serious, and I clocked her – pretty hard, harder than I meant – on the forehead. I suppose it was rather ungracious of me. . . .'

'But honour was saved?'

'She let go, at any rate. I put a foot against her chair, and shoved. It was on casters, so she went spinning halfway across the room. 'Please, please,' she implored, even then. 'It'll only take a minute, and I promise you'll enjoy – oh, my God, blood!' she shrieked. So I mopped her up as best I might – and here I am. I must say I feel awful about it. All sticky and beastly and hot. . . .'

'I'm not surprised,' I remarked sourly.

At my jaundiced expression Casilda laughed again. 'I wish I wasn't so squeamish, that's all,' she explained, and then added: 'I could dine with you tonight, if you like. Helen has gone away to the country. I deserve a really swell, slap-up dinner, don't you think, after what I've been through? Only I'm not a bit hungry . . . or let's just go to a movie. I'd quite as soon skip food. Oh, I've no idea *what* I want. That foul old bag ruined everything.'

'Try to forget all about it,' I said soothingly.

But Casilda had sunk into a reverie. She even ignored her tepid little drink, and sat bemused, staring into space. I mentioned half a dozen restaurants by name, and pushed the evening paper, with the list of cinemas, in front of her eyes. But they were fixed, vacantly, on a point past my right shoulder, and when at last she spoke, I could barely catch the words, they were uttered so softly, under her breath.

'Yes, I do, too – I know what I'd like. It's over there in the corner. Daddy, buy me that.'

I followed her gaze the length of the bar. At the other end, facing towards us with an evidently keen interest in Casilda, sat a hulking, swarthy young dago in a flamboyant brown suit, with vastly padded shoulders and an air of almost insolent admiration. Casilda, I am sorry to say, was giving him very much the same look in return.

'You can't mean that seriously,' I exclaimed – as a statement of fact, not a question. For one thing, he sported the sort of moustache that might have been drawn with an eyebrow-pencil an inch below his nostrils.

Casilda merely nodded, but as an affirmative

gesture it was all too definite. Any doubt in my mind was pure wishful thinking.

'I thought you said you didn't go in for gigolos,' I protested.

The girl gave a snort of mirth. 'Nor do I,' she agreed. 'But I can have this one for free, I assure you – if you'll let me. And you could watch,' she added in the same quiet tone, scarcely above a whisper. 'Wouldn't that excite you?' Her face was set, almost sullen.

There was silence between us for a moment. I needed time to think, to ponder this startling proposition. Without a word I paid the bill, kissed her cheek and walked out, bowing stiffly to the baffled foreigner, who hastily returned my salute with joyful bewilderment.

Was he any less puzzled on the back seat of the car, after an unceremonious introduction as 'My toreador,' while we drove towards Chelsea, with Casilda, happy and tense, nestling against my shoulder, her hand on my knee? He had a smattering of English – enough to gargle polite assent when Casilda asked him if this was his first visit to London, but her next question – 'Have you ever been kidnapped before?' – virtually drew a blank. 'Very pretty,' he assured us.

'Isn't he, though?' Casilda murmured, hugging my arm. 'He's a matador, you know,' she insisted.

'More like a picador, to judge by his looks,' I retorted. 'What are you going to do with this tough when you get him home?'

'The best he can,' said Casilda.

He chose whisky and accepted with alacrity an invitation from Casilda in French to be shown the house. I poured myself a big dollop of brandy, and settled down to read a couple of letters that the postman had brought. To this day I could not tell you what was in them. A few agonising minutes' wait was as much as I could bear.

They were not next door. She had led him off to the spare room upstairs – which was very considerate of her. He was kneeling with his back to me as I entered, his face pressed against her navel. She sat, naked to the waist, on the high four-poster, wih an arm around his bull neck, twisting his greasy curls. She took no notice of me whatsoever, and her conquest, oblivious of all else but the free gift of this magnificent body, did not even hear me come in. I lit the fire for them, and slipped into an easy chair near by to contemplate the scene.

He had evidently set about his business without a second's hesitation. The square, exaggeratedly masculine shoulders obscured her lower half from view, while his bent head was sunk in the hollow of her lap, and blindly, with both brown, hairy paws upstretched, he mauled, rather than fondled, Casilda's breasts. The way the fellow manhandled those sumptuous tits struck me as exceedingly rough and uncouth for a Latin lover: he plucked and tweaked and tugged at them, like some famished urchin snatching oranges from a tree. Nevertheless there was no sign of objection or complaint on her part; she kept her mouth shut tight and made not a sound, except for the fast, heavy breathing that shook her whole frame more violently from within, it seemed, than the harsh treatment to which this clumsy lout was subjecting her shapely facade.

She did not budge or flicker an eyelid. Yet if she, in rigid submission, might have withstood his bold assault indefinitely, it was clear that the hot-blooded Spaniard could brook no further delay. Muttering with impatience, the coarse creature sprang to his feet and started to tear the rest of her clothes off. She helped him then at once, promptly raising a docile backside to facilitate the complete removal of her rumpled dress and skintight panties, while she herself took off her fetching little suspender belt and stockings. As she leaned forward to do so, she suddenly, as I saw, undid his fly – and I too had the same impulse of unrestrainable curiosity, though for a different reason. What intrigued me was not Don Juan's credentials, but the effect they would produce on her. By craning my neck I caught a glimpse of her face, which revealed an expression of such sad and obvious disappointment that I probably let out a delighted guffaw. He spun round on me like a tiger, with eyes blazing fury at my intrusion. But his beautiful big dark eyes did not interest me; his erection did. It was rather short; not small, exactly, but a funny, fat, stubby instrument – a replica of the cocky young masher himself. His spitting image, I thought. Thick, I'll grant you – exceptionally thick, and to all appearance hard as marble.

Personally I am fairly large, even now, and

though of course comparisons are odious, I could sympathise with Casilda for taking such a dim view of his singularly unimpressive member. Certainly this was not the doughty Toledo blade by which she had expected to be smitten to the quick. It was stiff enough to fit her sheath, and stout enough to fill it adequately, but surely not long enough to pierce her very heart, as she had hoped.

In any case, this queer little blunderbuss was the last alarming weapon that our swashbuckling Spanish guest could brandish at me as he advanced in threatening fashion. I stood my ground, and watched him with some amusement.

'Go away from here!' he shouted, pointing towards the door. 'Madame and I will be alone.'

But Casilda rose up at that moment, like some vengeful goddess clad in the imposing plenitude of her pagan nudity, and summoned the hound to heel. She clung to the sleeve of his chocolate suit, restraining him. 'No, no!' she cried. 'Quiet, Carlos!' It was an order, rapped out sharply in the tone you would employ to subdue a ferocious mastiff, and she accompanied it with vehement shakes of the head, which he could not fail to understand. He hesitated, scowling in my direction, but she gripped him firmly by the convenient handle she found within reach and clamped her mouth on his, silencing his ugly splutters of rage. Barefoot, she was considerably the taller of the two, though no match for him in strength. He flung her back against the bed – but she held on to his penis firmly, so that he fell sprawling across her where she lay.

'No, no!' she cried once more. 'Not like that – naked like me. 'Hurry – take all this stuff off, quick!'

Hastily he obeyed her, stripping at full speed. He was as hairy as an ape. With a shock of surprise, I noticed that his shoulders were in fact immensely broad – no less broad than his natty suiting had made them out to be. Like Casilda herself, the brute looked better out of clothes. He was admirably built, I have to admit – as strong as an ox, evidently, and well shaped, with a deep chest and narrow hips, although too hirsute and too short of stature to qualify as an Adonis. But the general impression was of good, young male muscle beneath the thick coat of black fur which covered him like a rug from his neck to his ankles. It was only his genitals that were not up to much, by contrast, with the rest of his sturdy physique.

Casilda eagerly scrutinised this classical virile type while he undressed. Recining between the pair of carved, slender posts at the foot of the bed, where he had thrown her, for all the world like a goalkeeper alertly awaiting the next exultant forward rush, and with her eyes still riveted on him, it was then that she made the lewdest gesture I ever beheld in a lifetime of debauchery. Slowly, deliberately she stretched her long, lovely legs as far apart as she could spread them, doing the splits in that lolling position, so that we both – he and I – were confronted with a medical diagram of the vulva, highly coloured and fully extended, as in a textbook for students of gynaeocology. Not content with this obtrusive exhibition of her secret flesh, she turned exposure into invitation by offering him the target of her parted lips which she held open with two fingers in an inverted V for victory – or vagina.

For him it was an explorer's survey of the promised land, a preliminary viewing for his approval of the savoury dish that he had ordered. For me it was a blow across the face, a sudden, stinging shock of jealous horror. Until then my emotions had been mixed, uncertain, mostly dormant, as though by dint of will I had contrived to keep my feelings, if not under complete control, at least in abeyance. Curiosity and a shameful, vicarious excitement had usurped my normal faculties, numbing the spirit of revolt in my brain like a narcotic. Now, realisation of the vile role that I had assumed, both as pimp and cuckold, seeped over me, and a sweat of anguish broke out upon my brow. I was enveloped in some foul nightmare when I heard Casilda cry in the same urgent, raucous tone of imperative, intemperate desire:

'Come on now, man – take me! Give it to me! I want you.'

Before the words were out of her mouth he was inside her. He hurled himself forward into the open breach that was presented to him, as a battering ram of old must have crushed triumphantly through the weakened ramparts of an enemy citadel, vanquished and abandoned under siege. The impact winded her, and she uttered a loud gasp as the weight of the gorilla's vigorous onslaught knocked the breath from her body. His grappling hands dragged at her hips, pulling her half off the end of the bed, as he clambered upward, thrusting and jolting against her, jabbing and jerking, but at the same time holding her pelvis suspended in midair, as though to prevent the force of his attack from carrying her backwards, lest he should lose the prize he had seized or risk diminishing the violent contact of their private parts. I studied Casilda's face at this juncture, as she was lugged bolt upright into a sitting position by her arms, which were clasped behind his neck. She looked stunned, bereft, flabbergasted. Her eyes and mouth were as wide open as her legs, and fixed in a dazed expression. Rocked and pummelled amidships, she was beginning now to pant and strain in a wild attempt to draw the man down on top of her, so that she might herself enjoy the act in comfort, prone beneath his lunging bulk but solidly supported by the bed and able therefore to reply on even terms and keep her end up. He had gained the initiative; with his feet firmly planted on the floor, he seemed solely concerned to take his pleasure of her surrendered sex without scruple for his amorous partner's physical need, but seeking only to press home his own advantage over an all too easy victim.

My heart leaped for joy when I saw what was happening: this brash little dago was manhandling Casilda with the utmost rigour, he had roused her erotic instinct to fever pitch, he tupped her as savagely as a beast of the field – yet he could not satisfy her. He was using her merely as an object suited to his lustful purpose; but his very success in this selfish aim would prove a bitter blow to her – and she had asked for it. I was delighted to think that she was doomed to experience the direst disenchantment in my presence. Already I toyed with the idea of how I would upbraid her for this sordid and disgraceful display when it was over. If she was so wanton and so immoral as to hope that I might take the satyr's place, after he had finished with her, and carry on from where he left off, she would soon discover that she had made a big mistake. This was the end – I realised the fact with meridian clarity as I watched her lascivious antics in the arms of another man. I was through with Casilda Vandersluys for good and all. Directly after the fellow had gone, I would kick her out of the house. Or she could buzz off with him on her own if she liked – I didn't care.

Alas, how wrong I was! The mistake was entirely mine. I underestimated the dirty bastard – and the harlot who had picked him up, frankly preferring him to me, as casually as I might choose a whore in a brothel. She could not have guessed beforehand that he possessed such a small, stumpy tool which would scarcely fill the bill; but then neither could I foresee, at this initial stage of events, what stalwart use he would make of it, what fantastic feats of endurance the monster was capable of performing, how complete his victory would be, or what a shattering effect his persistence would have on so doughty an opponent as Casilda. She, I knew, was a tough nut to crack. I had marvelled at her reserves of energy and enthusiasm when she lasted through round after gruelling round with Helen. Keen as she was for the fray, Helen had not stood the pace to the finish with half so much in hand as the younger woman, who seemed wholly inexhaustible, ever ready to renew the engagement, gallantly impervious to fatigue. Casilda met more than her match in Carlos. His staying powers were incredible. Again and again he outlasted her, checking his own orgasm but making the randy bitch spend with increasing ecstasy each time, with longer, more profound, more exquisite spasms, by a delaying technique of extraordinary resilience which I never would have credited from hearsay.

Unfortunately for my peace of mind, it was not from hearsay that I learned the grim, incontrovertible truth of that young orangutan's sexual proficiency. To my chagrin and disgust I was obliged to witness the revolting demonstration of his prowess untiringly exercised on Casilda's wracked but willing frame, as it appeared to me, for hours on end . . . I was in agony throughout, yet powerless to prevent it. The experiment was conducted under my nauseated gaze – but there was nothing that I could do to stop the unspeakable cad from screwing my girl to distraction . . . and at her own request.

He started by his sliding both hands under her thighs and tearing them apart still further; then, when he had wrenched her open like an oyster, he pushed her knees back, bending them outwards as supplely as a frog's, so that he mounted her as if to probe her guts upon the operating table. She protested feebly, but her long legs were crossed high around his loins while he gradually ploughed his way deeper into her and farther up onto the bed. Eventually he had her flat on it, and she got a chance to retaliate in kind, battling against him hammer and tongs, as he crushed her under his weight and pounded her with his stiff, stout, chugging piston. For a time, as though moved by clockwork, he stuck to the same steady, regular, relentless rhythm, which was neither fast nor slow but evenly stressed, a succession of short, sharp stabs for many minutes at a time – until, not heeding Casilda's cries but of his own volition, to please himself, he would alter the tempo and shift the angle and the manner of his strokes. These tactical changes, occurring at odd intervals, swept all before him and soon reduced Casilda to an abject state of unassuaged, amazed submission. All tract of restraint, dignity or pride was gone. She had what she wanted – a surfeit of it, lashings of cock, almost more of the sweet physic than she could stomach. Well and truly was she getting laid; he poked her, decidedly, as she had never been poked before. The devil's pitiless prong sparked the molten red volcanic fires that consumed her burning crater and licked her entrails like subterranean tongues of flame. Tied to the stake, she wilted in the searing heat while he kept her there dangling upon the brink of an eruption, yielding to the protracted torture which she craved, yet yearning for the coup de grace to snap the unbearable tension of her nerves.

What the occupying force lacked in size, its seasoned spearhead, diligently employed, irrevocably entrenched, made up by aggressiveness. He humbled her twice, without succumbing himself, without the slightest sign of exhausion. Indeed he seemed annoyed by the readiness of her response, for on each occasion, as she neared the inevitable climax, he growled 'No, no, wait – not now, not yet!' when plainly she was incapable of obeying his command. Otherwise he seldom spoke, but uttered only a continuous series of guttural grunts while she, fainting in his arms, loose-limbed, tossing and floundering like a spiked fish, raved and moaned incessantly, repeatedly, through gritted teeth:

'Yes, oh yes, that's it, that's it, go on, yes, like that, go on, don't stop – ah yes, my God, dear God, don't stop, don't stop – you mustn't, oh Christ, now – ah – go on – more, more, oh please, no, don't stop, that's it – come on, you brute – oh God, yes, like that, damn you – ah, Jesus – you're killing me – go on, more – now, now, my God – I'm coming – I can't bear it – aah – now!'

They lay quiet, scarcely stirring for a while, but he did not withdraw. Hatred of them both sickened me; my knees were weak, escape or interference would be equally impossible, pointless; stricken with misery, anger and resentment, I retreated to my corner and slumped there, dosing my distress with brandy. The minutes slipped by. This disgusting farce had gone on long enough. Even

Casilda must have had her fill by now, and more, by the sound of it. I must tell her southern stallion that time was up, that he would have to leave, he need not think I had invited him to spend the night.

I was somewhat fuddled, but I had come to this drastic decision and was just getting ready to throw the blighter out – when they began again. He started rodgering her once more, for all he was worth, and she of course responded straightaway, putting her back into it, grinding and groaning as gladly as before. She was in luck. I doubt if anyone, in all her rich and varied experience, had ever screwed her so thoroughly. She was beside herself. For a girl who disapproved of blasphemy in bed – as I remember she had told me – some of the obscenities which she uttered now were, to say the least, appalling. I was shocked and revolted. Filthy endearments mingled in her mouth with invocations of the Almighty, animal noises, and muttered insults. Her scarlet nails, like talons, clawed at the ruffian's hairy back, scratching the humped, muscular neck, digging with bestial passion into his neat, bobbing buttocks. He growled, but manfully bore the sharp pain for a time, then – suddenly infuriated – he grabbed her by the throat, as if to throttle her, and raising himself, struck her savagely across the face, a stinging blow, with the flat of his hand.

Her mad, agonised grimace did not alter. But to me it was an outrage that was intolerable, a typical example of caddish violence that called for instant, chivalrous, condign retribution. I must avenge this maltreatment of a woman, if not the honour she herself had trampled or the respect which Casilda no longer merited. In attempting to do so, however, I tripped – or the young brute hit me, I'm not sure which – and I fell heavily against the fender, knocking my head. Before I could pick myself up – perhaps I was too slow, being somewhat dazed – that scoundrel of a Spaniard pounded upon me, as I lay there defenceless among the fire irons, unable to move. Quicker than lightning, he had ripped off my tie and fastened my hands with it securely beneath me. I aimed a kick at his midriff, but a dressing gown cord was knotted tightly about my ankles. I was trussed like a goose! He had no difficulty in hauling me onto my knees and toppling me backwards into the chair.

Limp and dishevelled, Casilda sat watching us from the bed. Her chin cupped in both palms, she looked listless and remote, a picture of dejection. I noticed that she did not raise a finger to help me, nor did she say a word, she was too haggard and cowed. When he turned to her again, she dropped meekly back to receive him in the same supine posture as before, with broad smooth thighs lifted above her navel . . . I remember nothing else from that moment on, except an aching glare behind the eyes. . . .

When I came to, a long time later, the pain was still there but the Spaniard had gone. Casilda was bending over me, her naked bosom in my face, as she untied my wrists, having already freed my feet. Somewhat belatedly she showed intense concern for my condition, and fussed over me like a devoted nurse who arrives on the scene of a childish accident after the harm was been done. I eyed her with derision and distaste. True to the innate, uncaring harlotry of all her sex, she gave not the slightest indication of remorse, regret or even consciousness of the enormity of her offence. She had been having a damned good time; it was over now, and that was that. Surely (her manner implied) I could not be so unreasonable and churlish as to begrudge her a little fun once in a while? After all, I had not stepped in and prevented it. Quite to the contrary, I had allowed her a free hand, for which she was prepared to be duly grateful, so long as I did not go and spoil everything by electing to grumble about a mere peccadillo that was best forgotten. How could I be so tiresome as not to realise that *our* relationship was far more important, whereas this business with the lecherous Spaniard was just a passing fling?

I believe in the sincerity of her innocent attitude towards what had taken place. She did not give it a further thought. Such honesty, even in a flaming whore, should be accounted a virtue. But I could not look on it in that light. My love and loyalty, my every emotion, my own manhood had been spurned, insulted, trodden in the dust. Jealousy flooded my brain like a raging torrent. Casilda was calmly putting on her clothes. She drank a sip of brandy out of my glass, and offered me the dregs.

'I'm so sorry, darling,' she said – but I could not tell exactly what she meant by the remark: she might have been apologising for the mere dribble she had left me.

'How many times?' I asked, through my fatigue, in a voice that may have sounded either casual or surly. She cast a glance at me and understood the question.

'Five in all, I think,' she answered. 'But I lost count.'

Half dressed, she came and sat cross-legged on the rug at my feet before the dying fire, which she dutifully replenished with a shovelful of coal. She braced herself for a postmortem – the errant school-girl or the housemaid expecting to be rebuked for breaking some valued knicknack.

'Do you know,' she said sadly, 'he only came twice? I always thought it was less easy for a man who is not circumcised to last out so long. One lives and learns.'

She had got into her stride. 'I must say he amazed me,' she added. 'But there it is. Phew! Give me an uncircumcised cock every time.'

I slapped her hard across the mouth, as he had done. The suddenness rather than the force of the blow sent her sprawling to the floor. She sprang up and faced me, spitting fury.

'You swine!' she snarled. 'You shit! How dare you? You filthy, drooling, dirty, impotent, goddam son of a bitch!'

There have been a few occasions in my life when I have lost my temper with some stupid woman – but never can I recall having been so shamelessly provoked, so wholly justified in the use of violence, as I then was by this crowing trollop. I will not deny that I enjoy a bout of playful flagellation now and again. I have spanked or whipped most of my mistresses at one time or another, for the fun of it. But this was different. I saw red. Her screeching abuse was more than I had bargained for. Strangling would have been too lenient, too quick a punishment for her, I felt. I snatched hold of her by the wrist and by the hair, I dragged her over to the bed, I clouted her again across the face and boxed her ears. She went on cursing me, pouring out a stream of shrill, inept invective against my righteous wrath when I left her there and rummaged through a chest of drawers downstairs for what was needed.

When I returned with a bamboo cane, she had not moved, but she fought like a wildcat to break away from my clutches, until I succeeded in turning her over by wrenching her arm round behind her back, while I knelt on her neck and other wrist, so that she was pinned facedown upon the bed, the furious tirade muffled by the pillows, and able only retaliate with kicking heels because I rolled the elastic knickers into a sort of rope or hobble binding the thighs tightly together, some little way below the bouncing buttocks. They leaped and shuddered and swung from side to side as I thrashed her with all my might, until the sound of her screams, muted as it was, could be heard above the whistling of the cane and the loud thud which signalled each stroke as if to count the crimson weals that marked the wonderful wide expanse of her arse in next to no time. I flogged her blindly at first, as I might have beaten a carpet – but the pattern of punishment, as it deepened and darkened in crisscross streaks, began to fascinate me, and soon I was drawing hieroglyphics in a methodical manner, with more art than sadism, on the taught, quivery canvas that bloomed like a peony. I decorated both cheeks equally with a design in purple, black and blue. When they opened with a supplicating, subconscious jerk, wincing apart as though split by a cruel swipe of my wand, I aimed a lengthwise cut along the smooth ravine itself, which shrank and shut again at once like the big, bulbous jaws of some strange, flustered sea monster. From her nape to her knees Casilda's back heaved, flinched, rippled and shook. It was a windswept yellow cornfield, poppy bright: bowed, tossed, flurried by the gale. It was an ice rink scarred by a thousand skaters' trails, a seething, swollen river lashed to livid turmoil at the storm's mercy. . . .

Mercy? She howled for mercy, but I gave her none. She could not escape; she must only endure. She should smart and bleed and faint, cringing and grovelling, while my wrath lasted. I flogged her till my arm grew tired. I relished her struggles, I joyed in her suffering, I got acute pleasure from inflicting extreme humiliation – where she would feel it most – on the incontinent flesh which she had yielded so readily, so wickedly, to another man in my presence.

I wish to emphasise again, however, that this pleasure for my part was physical perhaps, but not sexual. Her tail excited me: I trounced it for precisely that reason, in reverse – to cure myself of its attraction, not because I was jealous of the promiscuous slut, but simply to break her hold over me, to settle our account, to call it quits, and to teacher her a lesson. I would do no permanent damage to her naughty, burning backside; but if it ever forgot itself in the future, it must never forget me – the one lover who had missed his share of the lady's favours, yet had enjoyed her charms to his heart's content, by caressing them in his own special way. . . .

I let her go as soon as I was through – when I had lost interest in her wriggling, and felt she had been chastised enough. For me it was a sweet relief. I discovered that I no longer bore her any great grudge. It had simply had to be, and now it was done; I could rest easy, with the whole load of Casilda Vandersluys, a worthless burden, off my mind. It would be some time before she would care to flaunt her sorely bruised bum under Helen's nose or waggle it at any casual bedfellow, I reckoned – unless dignity mattered as little to her as decency. If she chose to make herself cheap, at least for a week or so, I'd turned her into a laughing-stock, highly coloured and comic; she could only indulge in intimacy at the risk of causing hilarity or actual ribaldry – and of providing me with a private joke in compensation. I flung the cane away across the room and fell asleep.

I do not know whether I awoke after a few minutes or an hour later, but the discomfort of wearing clothes prevented peaceful slumber. Casilda was still lying next to me, huddled on her side. I allowed her to doze on without interruption. She opened her eyes when I pulled the blankets over her and tucked her up for the night, but she did not speak or move, and her absent expression told me nothing of her feelings towards me. I undressed, tumbled into bed, and dropped off to sleep again instantly.

Daylight and the louder sound of traffic, or maybe the clatter of Mrs Howarth, the charwoman, barging about downstairs, gradually impinged on my consciousness and dragged me back to the realities of life which mankind coops for preference within four walls. But there was something else as well that I must have brought with me from the dreamless purlieus of a different, remote, forgetful world – a sense of serenity. I was awake, tranquil, refreshed – still drowsy, but peculiarly cheerful. Casilda lay curled in my arms, her head, a soft, fragrant nosegay of tousled chestnut tresses, on my shoulder. Assuming that she slept, I refrained with the utmost care from the slightest movement that might disturb her, even attuning every breath I drew to the tempo of her deep breathing. I conquered my intense desire to stroke and fondle the warm, firm, delicate flesh of the girl, lest my touch, however light, should rob her of the restful remedy that nature alone provides for rash extravagance.

So we remained, quietly locked in a tender embrace, for some time. But she, too, was feigning sleep, I realised, for when she stirred after a while, her hands glided with gentle stealth about my belly, caressing, fingering and finally clasping the emblems of power, the orb and sceptre of manhood, which she wielded silently but insistently until she was sure of me and satisfied with the result of her research, like the witch who knows that the love philter she has brewed is infallible in its effects. Then she spoke. In a murmuring voice that was low but distinct I heard her say:

'You're a fool, Tony, you know. You were wrong. But – never mind. I don't care. I love you. I really do. Not only now. Before. Only, it'll be still better now . . . you'll see. I'll show you. I had to make you wait . . . this is going to be the real time. . . .'

From nowhere her mouth burst out at me, engulfing mine, pressed to my lips like a hot, ripe fruit that is cool, thirst-quenching, sweet to the taste. In the next instant her body, an uncoiled spring, slid under me, beneath me, length for length, limb against limb. Her arms and legs were entwined about my body like ivy around a tree. . . .

'There, my love,' she said. 'Fuck me. D'you hear? I'm telling you now – fuck me.'

I plunged into her and dug my nails deeply into her belaboured buttocks.

'Go on,' she repeated. 'Fuck me!'

I had the incentive, and her command – and her. From that morning Casilda was my mistress. For both of us the long delay was over – and, as we had known in our hearts all along, the prize was worth it.

CHAPTER FIVE

Eve must have taken an enormous bite out of that apple, to keep us all munching away so happily on the fruity facts of life ever since. From the moment of our somewhat boisterous if belated entrance together into the Serpent's paradise, Casilda and I never looked back. We were both of us habitués of the place, in other company – but that rather enhanced than spoiled our mutual pleasure on revisiting those bright, vast, crowded though private domains where (as Casilda once observed of an amusement park) common-or-garden-of-Eden couples littler the lawns like nudists, literally two a penis.

The prolonged disquiet of the weeks spent in what I mighty wryly call my courtship of Casilda was forgotten. Sexually and in every way our idyll now seemed a marvellous thing to both of us. We made love like a pair of romantic youngsters or seasoned, vicious, veteran debauchees. We indulged in as many varied embraces as our few hours together allowed. It was still pretty difficult for us to meet, but whenever we got the chance we fell into each other's arms, however hastily and hurriedly – yet always with immense success. So regular and resounding was Casilda's appreciation that sometimes, satisfied (not to say satiated) as I was, a tiny suspicion lurked at the back of my mind that she might perhaps be exaggerating a bit, out of a wish to flatter my ego. Luckily I am not easy to deceive in such matters.

The approach of Christmas was fortunate – a favourable circumstance, abetting our designs. Helen shopped feverishly. Her daughter Cécile would be coming over for the holidays from her finishing school at St Cloud – and Casilda insisted on giving up her room to the girl. This tactful, tactical move to a different floor under the same roof would leave her more often to her own devices – and to mine. At heart Casilda's attitude towards her bosom friend had not changed, but Helen had been quick to detect the shining light of a new love in Cassy's eye, and if suspicion were not to become certainty she must dodge those intimate episodes that were naturally fraught with the danger of discovery, since any sign of diminished ardour on her part would blow the gaff as surely as an open confession. So long as she could avoid getting to grips, Casilda might be able to bamboozle the

Baroness, whom she was anxious to hoodwink – for her own sake – while our affair lasted.

Not that either of us had the slightest inclination to end an absorbing experiment which we were only now starting to conduct in earnest. We were ideally suited to each other by temperament. I had not suspected the existence of a masochistic streak in Casilda until I hit upon it, so to speak, purely by accident; hitherto, in the course of all her confidential chatter, she had never so much as hinted at this pleasing kink which added, for me, to her attraction. I freely acknowledge that it appealed to an answering though latent impulse of sadism in myself that I had always done my best to restrain, lest it develop from an innocuous whim into a positive obsession which I should find both troublesome and difficult to gratify. Not since the first careless raptures of my salad days had I enjoyed sexual intercourse so blithely, so intensely as now, on the brink of fifty, with a partner so adept, versatile and willing as Casilda. This was unquestionably as rewarding and splendid a liaison as any rake could wish to preserve among a stock of comforting memories laid by for his old age. Casilda had and did everything it would ever enter my head to demand of a mistress. To my way of thinking, she was frankly perfect.

But perfection, we know, is not of this world. There must always be a 'but' – for true love ends swiftly in boredom if its course runs smooth, and you do not need to be a cynic to realise that this in fact is what the tellers of fairy tales mean when they say the bridal pair 'lived happily ever after.' It's a catchphrase with a catch in it. Matrimony, monogamy and monotony are synonymous, marked by the most melancholy of initial letters. No such morbid menace hung over us, of course; the risk of marriage did not arise. Yet there was a fly in the ointment, I was dismayed to find. The thought of Helen's lasting hold upon Casilda haunted me even now that I had made the grade and won a temporary victory over our wardress. It was an altogether ludicrous situation – but I was horribly jealous of Helen. My charming affair with Casilda was developing right from the start into a sharp-angled triangle.

It did not take Helen long to smell a rat, though she had not guessed that the rat was myself, Anthony Grey. Her intuition warned her something was afoot – and amiss – but she still had no clue to her rival's identity, although I believe she was shrewd enough to read the signs of Casilda's deep-seated contentment as the handiwork of a member of the opposite sex. Puzzled and worried as she was, she put a brave front on her misery and went out of her way to conceal it from Casilda, on whom she now lavished affection and sweetness, presumably in the hope of shaming her into making a clean breast of this latest infidelity, which she knew to be more serious than usual.

'I've no doubt she's being extra nice and kind to you at present,' I sneered, when Casilda stood up for her soul mate. 'But just wait till she discovers who is cuckolding her. She'll scratch your eyes out

106

straightaway – and I shall be made to suffer for it too, you may be sure, even if it takes her the rest of her life to get even with me. Helen can be horribly spiteful. She's going to have to forgive you in the long run, but she'll see me in hell first. She hates my guts, as it is.'

'What utter nonsense you talk! You really couldn't be more wrong,' Casilda testified heatedly. 'As a matter of fact she has quite a soft spot for you, although you always do your best to provoke and annoy her. Besides which, you must understand that Helen would only need to be jealous of you if you were half your age. At twenty-five or thirty she would recognise you as an appalling threat to my virtue – and to her sacred right of ownership – as either suitor or seducer. You might wrest me away to the altar or carry me off as your plaything, if we were blinded by youthful passion. At our time of life the odds are against either of us being so rash or so irresistible. However desperately they may fall for one another, she argues, they are certain to get over it before long. She regards you as a professional philanderer – extremely presentable, but on his last legs where women are concerned. She told me so herself, quite recently.'

'How good of her! But she only said that to test your reaction.'

'Not in the least, I promise you. She's neither such a simpleton nor so complicated and hypocritical as you like to think, but a mixture – like most of us. You shocked her profoundly that night at dinner by your insinuation of untold vice

– but you intrigued her too, of course. You repel and attract her at the same time, just as Lucien used to in the old days. There's nothing extraordinary about that, to a woman's turn of mind. You're her type.'

'Well, I'll be damned! You don't suppose I'm tickled pink to hear that the Baroness has this weakness for me, do you? Or to be compared to a fat and filthy old wreck like Lucien? Let them stew in their own juice, blast them! I would rather not pursue the subject.'

We were lying snugly in bed together on a foggy evening in December. A few minutes before this wrangling conversation began, we had been locked in each other's arms, giddy and choking with delight like swimmers battling happily in the surf of a tumultuous, exultant passion. The strong tide of our desire had receded, leaving us limp but thankfully at rest on a tranquil, firm and sunny shore. In a moment it would be time to get up, to dress and refresh ourselves, to sally out into the raw night for dinner. I lay at ease, sipping my whisky, as I watched Casilda stretch, like a great sleek marmalade cat, and bound in a couple of strides through the door to the bathroom. She would return, I knew, to warm her radiant body before the fire and then, with leisurely gestures, while she discussed where we should sup or prattled about trivial topics, she would don an enticing array of flimsy little garments, allowing me plenty of time to appraise each frill and flounce, every clinging curve, rotundity and crease, as though

108

performing a striptease act in reverse for my delectation.

It was one of those good occasions which Casilda called her 'Cinderella sprees,' as distinct from the quick, birdlike encounters in mid flight that most often had to suffice us by way of love-making, now that Casilda had exchanged her previous strategy of insufferable delays for a direct approach of uncompromising speed. Tonight was an exception: she could easily get home ahead of the Delavignes, who would be late back from some pompous party. She was aware of my special penchant for dainty lingerie, which did indeed amount almost to a fetish in my case and she indulged it to the fullest, out of the kindness of her heart, whenever there was an opportunity to stage the sort of peep show that I can happily feast my eyes on for hour after hour. I don't believe I ever saw her parade the same scanties twice; she must have owned a vast wardrobe of these ravishing pieces of intimate finery that lend additional temptation to the naked truth, forming a gay disguise to deck out the bare facts, as it were, with an ethereal smile, a trace of mystery which is not meant to fool the onlooker but only to enhance the beauty of each succulent morsel, like the sugar coating on crystallised fruits. In her dressing and undressing Casilda was about as spectacular as a Parisian revue. From the simplest and sheerest to the most fanciful and elaborate, from naughtiest nylon to softest wool, all the decorative variety of feminine underwear in every shape and shade, from the amply old-fashioned, starched and rustling, to the tightly stretched, close-fitting modern style of millinery, my delicious mistress had the whole wanton lot – a galaxy of bows, lace, ribbons, tucks and folds adorning every kind of froufrou, from bloomers to briefs, from petticoats and knickers to panties and slips, cat's-cradle bras and girdles, garters and *guepières.* . . .

I was watching the display no less avidly than usual when a dark suspicion fell like a chill, deep shadow across my mind, as though on a bright summer afternoon a cloud out of the blue sky had suddenly obscured the sun. Jealousy's first stab strikes often in this way, by stealth, like some dread disease. It was then, at a careless moment, while Casilda moved in silhouette against the playful glow of the firelight, that I was struck by a new doubt and recognised the symptoms of further and worse pain to come. Why are we by nature so perverse that our profound pleasure in a woman's sexual experience is undermined at once and blighted by the mere thought of how she must have acquired it? What fools men are to resent the bygone joys that have possessed this body which they now love, and to cavil at those other unknown males who moulded and instructed in the service of Venus! Innocence and chastity appeal only temporarily to an aggressive masculine instinct that derives acute personal satisfaction but no permanent solace from destroying them, and though the seducer himself rejoices at their loss on that unique occasion, it will be mourned and regretted thereafter by not a few of his successors. Blazing the trail, this favoured pioneer stakes his triumphant claim to scalped virginity, for he snatches that invaluable first prize, at one swoop, from all who follow in his wake, yet he will reap nothing in due course but their recurrent envy and hatred. Nevertheless he has served a useful purpose; we must be grateful to him at least for saving us a fair amount of trouble. It is our many other predecessors, down the long line of bedfellows, who incur our maledictions. Who were they to tamper with our chosen property, which ought to have kept intact, fresh and unspoiled, for us? By what right did they dare lay their foul, interfering paws on these objects of delight, which we were destined someday to want? Yet, after all, their crime is understandable: we would have done – and in fact have done – the same thing ourselves, giving not so much as a fleeting thought to those who afterwards will tarry, seeking shelter in this selfsame cosy spot. But she, the woman in the case – ah, there is the horror and the shame of it! – how could she? What vanity, what crazy aberration, rendered her always so prompt, so ready to yield without demur to such an innumerable procession of gross, unworthy lovers? Here is the guilt, the villainous offence, the insult heaped upon frolics with Tom, Dick and Harry. They were quite right to take advantage of the opening she offered, the randy slut, to all and sundry, like a bitch in heat, mounted by every dirty dog in turn, with lolling tongue, at the street corner.

Lucien! The name struck me like a knife between

the ribs. Of course! How could I have been such a fool as not to realise it before? His ugly face, with its moles or warts, its sallow, heavy jowl and brilliant beady eyes, loomed in my memory, and I pictured his gesture of stroking his Roman emperor's nose with a crooked forefinger as he talked, smiling sardonically. Ugh, yes – he must have had her too. Repulsive creature! The very idea made me feel sick. He was the perfect storybook ogre, complete with a wife of wondrous beauty – who had inspired more than her due of passionate jealousy in me, as I now saw. I was beginning to commiserate and side with her, for no doubt she, poor woman, had suffered as much as I when she discovered who had been her chief rival in Casilda's arms. Possibly I had less cause for complaint than Helen, since Lucien's fling with the girl must date back a goodish while. Then why on earth could Casilda not have told me, with her usual honesty, that she was involved with both the Baron and the Baroness, instead of only one of them, far the more handsome of the pair? Perhaps that explained Helen's reported friendliness towards me. There was a bond between us, even though she might not know it – a fellow-feeling, subconscious probably, if she were truly ignorant of my connection with Casilda, but telepathic, genuine and valid nonetheless . . . maybe, after all, she was not so impervious to consolation as Cassy made out. Helen and I already had something in common, it seemed. You can never tell with emotional entanglements of this sort. In time she might wish to shift her position

and ally herself with me, if only to share my
vengeance upon her faithless husband and the
deceitful hussy who had wronged us both. Who
would have thought it? Casilda, who claimed to
keep no secrets from me, had let me down here
badly by slyly, deliberately omitting to confide that
she had slept with Lucien, of all people, who was
the central and certainly the most important figure
in our scheme of things.

'A penny for them, darling.' Casilda's cheerful
challenge broke in, from a distance, on my grim
meditations.

'I was wondering how you could bear to live
under the same roof as Lucien – even for Helen's
sake,' I answered.

'Oh, Lucien is not much trouble,' Casilda
remarked indifferently, adjusting a shoulder strap.
'Everyone agrees that he's extremely witty and
amusing. What has he done to put you against
him? You used to say you admired the old rascal.'

'He's astute and altogether unscrupulous, that's
all. I consider his flair for art impressive – but
we've never been close friends. And I don't like the
sentimental tone in which you refer to him, as
though he was your favourite uncle or your elder
brother – the black sheep of the family but an
absolute dear who means no harm by it really.'

Casilda laughed. 'Oh, pooh!' she said. 'Lucien
has his faults . . . but he's not a prig. Just a bit of
a scamp.'

There was a long pause that bristled with conjec-
ture, while I glared at the half-clothed, taunting

figure by the fire. She seemed disposed to prevaricate indefinitely. Her raised eyebrows and the quizzical, mischievous smile mocked me until I was forced to blurt out the direct question:

'Do you deny having gone to bed with Lucien?'

'Of course not, Tony. But it was ages ago – five or six years at least. You knew that, surely.'

'How should I have known? Damn you,' I said, 'you never told me.'

'Well – it's such an obvious thing to happen. I assumed you must have guessed,' Casilda blandly declared.

'So jolly simple for Lucien, you mean,' I jeered. 'Trust your benefactor, such a sportsman, not to miss the sitting bird. And you made it nice and easy for him. I expect – out of gratitude for his hospitality.'

Leaning with one elbow on the mantlepiece, Casilda eyed me calmly but said nothing.

'Exactly what took place?' I asked, finally. 'When, and how? I insist on hearing the whole nasty story.'

Casilda laughed aloud again at the sight of my distress.

'Darling!' she cried. 'If only you could see yourself! There's no need to despair – you can relax. It wasn't serious, I promise you. I'll tell all – if I can remember the details. It's so long ago. But please take that suicidal look off yor face. I was rather naughty – we both were, I admit – but not half so appallingly wicked as you seem to imagine. Actually the first time was quite funny. . . .'

'Go on,' I snapped. 'I'm sure it was – great fun. Both of you have a highly developed sense of humour. But I wonder if Helen saw the joke.'

'She mightn't have,' Casilda agreed. 'Tell her, and you'll find out – if she believes you. We went to bed with her, you see – all three of us together – but she never noticed what happened.'

'I warn you: don't lie to me.'

'I'm not lying. Cross my heart – it was soon after I first went to spend a few weeks with them one winter, and they had asked me to stay on. They lived in Hampstead then. I had been in the house about six months. I was just over eighteen. They treated me like a daughter, and encouraged me to regard the place as my own home, because it was the only one I had. Sometimes, especially on Sundays, I would carry my tray into their room and have breakfast with them. That morning we were recovering from a very late night before. It was the Season, and we had been dancing until the early hours. We were all still practically asleep, and when I complained of feeling chilly Helen suggested I should get into their big bed for warmth. She was reading through a pile of Sunday papers, while Lucien dozed. I got in on his side of the bed and curled up with a novel. Lucien lay with his back to me, next to Helen, who sat propped up against pillows and buried in the *Observer*. I was only half awake when, after a bit, Lucien turned over to face the same way as me. He snored intermittently but scarcely stirred – until a hand beneath the bedclothes unfastened my bathrobe and moved

115

gently about my body. Its touch was deft and exciting; soon I was having the greatest difficulty keeping still and not giving the game away. At such close quarters the least little wriggle, the faintest gasp would catch Helen's attention at once; she couldn't fail to recognise signs which, however slight, are all too unmistakable. . . . Lucien by now had edged up behind me, pressing hot and hard against my tail end, which he bared very gradually and surreptitiously, an inch at a time . . . I did not help him at first, while he pulled my robe and nightie up at the back and tucked them out of the way, around my waist – but the next stage was the trickiest part of the proceedings, it took a good deal of care, patience and self-control for us to manoeuvre safely into the right position. Lucien had the beginnings of a paunch on him, even in those days, and I was obliged to bend far forward – with the utmost caution, holding my breath – before there was any hope of achieving our aim. When we managed it at last, and he started to slide into me – at a snail's pace, and just as silently – I nearly had to lean out of bed, though we still didn't dare betray the steady progress of our increasingly lively sensations by so much as a sign or a shudder . . . the strain was devilish. I don't know if you've ever undergone any similar experience – but think what it's like, not being able to risk a single brusque movement, far less let yourselves go, either of you, even when deep down inside you're coming closer and closer, faster and faster, to the absolute core of hectic mutual pleasure. We had to stay dead quiet

– as innocent on the surface as babes in the wood, while below, under the sheets, we were joined and welded by a raging fire that knotted us tightly together at the hub of a rigid figure K – which became an X finally, as we reached our secret spasm. And that didn't take long, I can tell you – the double effort of motionless energy was overwhelming, it heightened the tension somehow by concentrating every ounce of feeling at the centre, the focal point. . . .'

'The fulcrum – that is the correct term,' I appended. 'And then what?'

Casilda had dressed while she was talking. She came and planted an affectionate kiss on the top of my head.

'Nothing much else, honey,' she assured me. 'There were a few other episodes, at intervals over the next couple of years, but none of them important. Always at some unguarded moment, though, when you least expected it, in the most peculiar circumstances. Lucien liked it better that way. He was pretty near impotent already. I suppose he needed the spice of variety – but there's no question about it, he certainly has the dirtiest instincts. He's not just lewd but downright obscene. I don't remember his ever satisfying me entirely except that first time, when I was young and eager and felt we were being frightfully wicked. The next incident, I think, was in the bathroom, before a big dinner party they were giving. He sometimes walked in and chatted to me while I was taking a bath – even with Helen in the offing. But it meant nothing to him; what he wanted was to watch me on the can. This gave him a terrific kick – he adores seeing girls pee, especially in the open, squatting down to it, with skirts up and knickers round their ankles, in a ditch or a field. Widdling on the loo was tame by comparison, but he often begged one to indulge his 'silly fad' by doing that – or the other thing. I drew the line at that. I don't mind making water in front of anybody, if it amuses them – but I'm not prepared to go further. Scatological foibles revolt me, I'm afraid. Lucien's particular whim was to urinate between one's legs, aiming the stream at one's clitoris. He tried it on me that evening, and then insisted on playing "sweet little Cassy's nurse" who scrubs her in the bath. He soaped me all over and attempted to take me, slippery as an eel, under the shower. It wasn't a great success – so in the end he sat on the stool and got me to straddle his lap as widely as possible while he rubbed himself off against me. The trouble was we had to hurry – Helen would be along in a jiffy – and gambols of this kind depend on trial and error. Still, he got what he was after, and it didn't really bother me.'

'Evidently not. You appear to have enjoyed yourself considerably.'

'Well, yes, I suppose so – but I couldn't raise a shindy and refuse him, could I? Besides, it did sometimes suit a passing mood . . . he's excessively ardent when roused, but not in the least maudlin. I like sex on those terms. He understood me. We always got on well together.'

118

'Is that so? Then why did you give up sleep with him, may I ask?'

'I'm telling you – it wasn't exactly an affair. I mean, we only actually went to bed that once. He didn't want me in the normal way. He infinitely preferred the sneaking, hole-in-the-corner business of sudden odd grabs at you every so often. Except for an occasional savage pinch or some leering remark, he didn't pester me again for months after the bathroom scene. But embarrassing situations were meat and drink to him. One day, for instance, he slipped a hand up under the skirt of an extremely pretty little thing in the drawing room – she was a guest who had arrived early for lunch at the house – and he went on playing with her while I poured the drinks and rearranged the flowers. "Keep a lookout at the window for Helen," he told me. The child was blushing like a beetroot, though she was a forward young piece, the daughter of a peer, and as vicious as a monkey. Lucien talked the whole time without stopping – a spate of the most outrageous remarks in the manner of a running commentary, comparing the two of us and excusing himself to the girl for not pleasuring her properly, he said, because I had exhausted him in my room just before she turned up. She should take lessons from me, he explained, I was incredibly gifted, a world-famous authority, second to none in such matters. He described our relative anatomical advantages and suggested the correct use for them in such lurid detail that we both burst out laughing. She slapped him for his impertinence at one

119

moment, and stuffed her fingers in her ears, but she was giggling so helplessly I was afraid she might have hysterics. Helen was quite mystified when she came in to find us all sniggering like idiots.

'Another time I went into Lucien's study and there he was, necking Helen's French maid on the sofa. He sprawled back, pretending not to notice my presence, and pushed Suzette down on the floor between his knees. But she shook him off and darted out of the room like a scalded cat as soon as she saw me. "Pity," Lucien grumbled. "She has just the mouth for it. . . . Never mind, dear, you'll do nicely instead – it was your fault, barging in and disturbing us." Like a sultan or some randy old raja he looked, lying among the cushions, languidly waving his tool at me – or maybe more like a snake-charming Eastern beggar, flapping that long, limp thing around, though it was I who had to toot the tune and do his ropetrick for him. . . .'

'You of course consented out of sheer kindness?'

'Uh-huh – after a bit of persuasion, to avoid a fuss.'

'I hope he was duly grateful. How often were you called upon to perform these trifling favours? Presumably he repaid them?'

'I'd gladly have overlooked the debt, given the option. But he did go down to me, as a matter of fact, on at least two occasions – though I fought to prevent it one evening, waiting in the car outside a nursing home, while Helen visited a sick friend. It was a fairly dark street, but she would be with us again in a minute, we were hideously uncomfortable, needless to say, and I was as nervous as a nun – it seemed we'd never finish! Lucien simply refused to stop or listen to reason, and my futile pretence at an orgasm he ignored as pure trickery – which it was. What a nightmare!'

'Who won?'

'Well, really he did, more or less – in the very nick of time. He always got away with it, Lord knows why. But what is the good of resisting, if one is going to have to give in eventually? He damn nearly strangled me on a country stroll once, behind a haystack, because I did my best to fob him off with a frigging when he demanded a gamahuche. . . . He had the whip hand over me. It wasn't so terrible, after all – was it?'

There was a pause. Casilda hovered at my side, inquiringly.

'It is rather a scabrous story, I admit,' she said. 'But I wasn't quite as awful as you thought, was I? Are you going to forgive me?'

'Your effrontery is colossal – and your attitude as indecent as it could be, if you want my opinion. Utterly deplorable, even for you – and in such bad taste! The blame is yours, more than Lucien's, I'm convinced.'

Casilda smiled. 'You know what I'm like, Tony darling,' she murmured, and then, after gazing at me fondly in silence: 'Shall I fetch the stick, my lord? I realise I deserve it.'

At my nod, she went to the chest of drawers, remarking lightly: 'The bottom drawer, I assume?' and a hint of anxiety crept into her voice as she added, 'this one?' handing me the long, fine, flexible malacca cane.

I pointed to the armchair by the fire. 'Bend over,' I ordered sharply. An anticipatory thrill of harsh excitement mingled with the dull ache of my jealous indignation and disgust. Casilda knelt in the chair, resting her elbows on the back, and waited. 'Not too hard – please, darling,' she entreated quietly, as I rolled her dress up above her waist and gently, deliberately undid her full, frilly panties, which stayed in place and had to be pulled down, inch by inch, over her hips. I took my time about these preparations – for me more enjoyable and satisfying than the subsequent infliction of corporal punishment, whereas for the victim herself perhaps enduring the ordeal may prove pleasanter by far than the preliminary suspense attached to it. Thus I toyed with the intention of removing her frail satin girdle, but left it to form a saucy frame, like a flowered border, around the rich, broad, beautiful view of her buttocks.

'I shan't whip you,' I volunteered, 'if you regret your decision. Only say so now, before it's too late. Cry off at once, if you feel so inclined – but don't give me instructions. You'll get what's coming to you.'

Casilda shook her head, and buried her face in her arms. 'I can take it,' she asserted, 'if you'll promise to drop the subject after this. That's the bargain – a solemn tabu on all further recriminations about Lucien.'

'Kiss the rod,' I commanded.

'Curse you,' she said, complying. 'You mean, miserable bully!'

She glanced at me over her shoulder with a steely-grey, inimical glint in her big hazel eyes. So it was not bravado, she was not putting it on. Her face was deathly pale, but I would not have liked to swear that she was frightened, despite the trace of a tremor on her lips and a certain glassy look belying her defiant tone. After the first half-dozen strokes, however, there was no longer any doubt . . . they landed with a loud swish and thwack across her ruddy rump, each echoed by a piercing yelp. Gnawing her knuckles, biting her own sleeve as a gag to muffle a series of pitiful howls and strident shrieks, she soon shed all hypocrisy and implored me to lay off.

'That'll do! Stop, stop! Tony! Oh! Ah! Ow! Ow-uuh!'

Her hands now had broken loose – fluttering, clutching, clawing the air, snatching spasmodically behind her back in timid attempts to parry the blows; they flinched, recoiled, were whisked away yet returned in self-defence as I gradually increased the vigour of the thrashing, which even so was far less severe than the flogging she got on that impudent Spaniard's account the time before. Lucien was no stranger, after all, but an old, evil acquaintance of mine.

I lammed into her, but she shielded her bottom and swung around in sobbing supplication on the chair. There was nothing else for it: I had to seize her by the middle and lug her down over my knee.

I slid my hand beneath her then, and thrust it between her thighs. To some extent my touch was soothing . . . my fingers were intrumental in assuaging the wretched girl's pain . . . they were buried and burned in a fiery furnace, seeking an antidote, a balm to compensate for the heat of the hiding. In a few moments the cure was almost complete. Casilda spread her legs and stuck her arse out eagerly, clamouring for more of the treatment in stronger doses, like a wonder drug. . . .

'Harder!' she shouted. 'Yes, yes – that's it, harder! Beat me – oh – darling – harder. . . . No . . . Aah! As hard as you like. . . !'

CHAPTER SIX

'Opera, yes, opera – at Covent Garden,' Casilda
patiently repeated, on the telephone next morning,
as though to a backward child. 'I forgot to mention
it last night, with all the fuss . . . a treat for Cécile
– she's off to Paris again on Saturday. You're to
meet us in the foyér, if you don't mind . . . because
they'll have an awful rush getting up from Sussex
in time. Wasn't there a note in the post for you
from Helen?'

'No – and I shan't accept, anyway,' I answered
shortly.

'Why not? Darling, don't be so stuffy! You swore
to bury that little old hatchet, for one thing – and
for another, you shouldn't miss this *Aida*. Or Cécile,
either – however much it bores you to sit through
an opera. She's quite a dish, our Cécile, at sixteen.
I assure you. The picture of innocent youth, as

fresh as a peach – really lovely. You won't be able to take your eyes off her – I can't.'

'Who else has been asked?'

'There'll just be the five of us. I suggested including you. Sorry, darling.'

'What for? It sounds a swell party – almost a royal flush of your dearest friends. I suppose you fixed it like that as a joke – the queen with her court of four lovers, all in a row.'

'No, not in a row, stupid – Lucien's taken a box. Honestly, Tony, you're worse than incorrigible. That's an idiotic crack, quite uncalled-for and you know it. How dare you imply that I've meddled with Cécile in any way, or even thought of such a thing? Poor kid, she's angelic! Nobody but a fiend would lay a finger on her. Your mind is an absolute sink!'

'Oh, I don't know. Someone will, before long – if they haven't already. You'll see. Most maidens of Cécile's age look purer than snow, but a lot goes on under that icy exterior. Still waters run deep, I've discovered.'

'Well, there's nothing doing, get that straight – I forbid *you* to take the plunge in this case.'

'I won't – you needn't worry. I leave the whole of that family to you, my sweet. They're your pigeons. But it would be the nicest possible revenge for me, don't you think, if I succeeded in seducing Lucien's only daughter? I might be tempted to try my hand at it for that reason, as a matter of elementary justice. Somebody's got to do the job, Cassy darling: it would be a bit tricky, I fear, in a

126

box at the opera. And she's leaving London next day. . . .'

Casilda had hung up on me. She was out when I telephoned later to accept Helen's invitation. It amused me that she, bless her heart, should affect to be so shocked, when I had only meant to tease her. The cheek of the girl! Imagine such an incontinent hussy cavorting on her high horse, as priggish as you please, because I chose to jest about her precious little protégée's virginity! Women are wonderful. Obviously she must be harbouring fell designs of her own on the virtue of Mlle Delavigne . . . one might almost conclude that the charming adolescent stood in need of my gentlemanly protection. . . .

I was weary of these constant quarrels, however, and determined to enjoy my affair with Casilda. It was too profitable and pleasant a setup to ruin by rash outbursts of temper or disagreement over trifles. If Casilda's attitude to certain emotional issues seemed niggling and petty, I must not allow myself to be drawn into a battle of wits which I should only win to my own cost. I wasn't going to let a silly schoolgirl come between us – even if Casilda really was interested in her sexually, which on sober reflection seemed extremely improbable. She had enough on her plate, as it was, and anybody further removed from the hungering, hard-bitten, predatory type of lesbian would be difficult to imagine. It ought to be possible to enlist her aid, once she calmed down and emerged from her huff – if I tackled the problem in the right way.

From Casilda's description of little Miss Delavigne, vengeance in this particular case would taste sweeter than usual . . . surely the best plan would be to join forces, when the time came, and launch a combined attack. . . .

She was a peach, all right – with a liberal portion of clotted cream to soften the vivid colouring she inherited from both her parents. She had their raven-black hair and big velvety eyes, Lucien's dark skin rather than Helen's pallor, but the contrasting glow of Helen's red lips and a rosy bloom of health on her young cheeks in lieu of Lucien's sallow tint and somewhat oily complexion. Impeccably fashioned on the simplest lines, like its wearer, her modest evening dress of girlish pink encased the slight, slim figure from bosom to shin and showed it off for precisely what it was worth, without any vain attempt to hide or to improve it. Her demeanour matched her dress, lending her an air of elegance without sophistication, for she was as beautiful and as smart in appearance as her mother, but neither shy nor precious – a dignified and distinguished child, reserved and serene in manner, yet endowed, as one gathered from her few but intelligent remarks, with the makings of Lucien's mundane wit and artistic taste in replica. Paris, too, had done wonders for her. I did not recognise the bashful brat I sometimes came across at Regent's Park only a couple of years previously. Here was a full-fledged junior miss, typical in many ways, but exceptionally pretty — a ravishing specimen of girlhood, if the truth be told – and possessed of the great gift that such creatures normally lack: individuality.

Despite all this – or perhaps just because it was such a very highly polished product – I did not greatly take to Cécile. She made the same effect on me at first as her mother always had, until quite recently. My opinion of Helen had gained considerably in warmth since I had started to trick her with Casilda. Her daughter, I was grieved to see, left me as cold as frozen lamb. I admired Cécile's delicate profile, her regular features, her straight back and the low, melodious tone of her voice, as I sat leaning forward in the box at Covent Garden between her and Helen – but it was the latter who attracted me and stole my attention entirely. We were in W formation, with the three women in front. Lucien, beside me, had closed his eyes and slumped in his chair, listening to the music as soon as the lights were dimmed; halfway through Act I, he was snoozing. Casilda, to my right, had greeted me most curtly on arrival and now turned a bare cold shoulder on me with such studied insolence that I could have slapped her, although inwardly amused by this meaningless display of dudgeon, which did not perturb me in the slightest. I envisaged no serious risk of our breaking off the affair so soon, we were both still much too keen on each other; this nonsense on her part was only a lovers' tiff, engineered as the prelude to a passionate reconciliation. But I wasn't having any, thank you. I didn't need the tonic she was trying to prescribe for added ardour. It surprised me, on the contrary, as I would have thought she'd had all the spanking she could want for the time being. . . .

Helen, by contrast, was exceedingly amiable. I had never known her in a friendlier mood. She apologised profusely for not inviting me to dinner, and her attitude throughout our whispered conversation was singularly forthcoming. It struck me that her nonchalance towards Casilda was equally marked. Why so gay and gushing? I asked myself. What was her object in singling me out tonight particularly, under Cécile's very nose, as such a special favourite? She was as merry as a cricket and – one would almost suspect – positively flirtatious. I could only assume she was jealous and that she acted in this way to spite the faithless Casilda. Granting for the sake of argument that she was indeed as well disposed towards me as Casilda made out, would she have chosen this unpropitious occasion to reveal a weakness which could scarcely be acknowledged, let alone requited in public? She must merely be trying it on, I decided. Her idea was to provoke Casilda into a tantrum that would give the game away, by setting her cap at me while the going was good, in absolute safety. . . .

I saw that I was being used as a decoy. Helen had rather a fancy for me, and she welcomed this opportunity to indulge it, at Casilda's expense, in order to flick her on the raw and find out for certain if Anthony Grey was the nigger in the woodpile. Casilda wasn't saying a word . . . very well then: she would take this potshot in the dark to see how much I meant to her chum. Whether Casilda reacted with tell-tale annoyance or not, she was sure to be deeply riled by the experiment – and that suited Helen down to the ground, even if it left her still in doubt as to which of us, herself or I, was the chief cause of Casilda's irritation and jealousy. It was a gambit, Helen must have felt, by which she had absolutely nothing to lose.

No more had I, come to that. There was hay to be made, since the sun shone so brightly. Maybe I was emboldened to take advantage of this totally unforeseen situation by the number of whiskies I had consumed, in place of food, to fortify myself for the ordeal of an evening at the opera. Certainly I have no precise recollection of how it all began, and only the haziest memories of what was happening on the stage at any turn of the drama which I privately produced and played out, with a limited cast of two, before an oblivious or somnolent audience in our plush box above the footlights. The first I knew was that my hand came casually in contact with the beautiful bare back of the dear Baroness, that it rested there awhile before starting to stroke the firm flesh, from the nape of the slender neck to the pronounced curvature at the waist, and afterwards lingered soothingly between the shoulder blades, on the plausible pretext of plucking idly at the fur that hung over the chair upon which I leaned, supporting my elbow in rapt attention to Verdi's true lovers singing their sweet duet. Helen's vermillion satin dress was wonderfully naked, except for the huge spray of white orchids that sprouted from her bust in such profusion that its purpose as a corsage might have seemed more practical than ornamental, to cover her bosom for the sake of decency rather than merely to embellish it as flamboyantly as possible.

She sat stock-still, without moving a muscle, I was happy to note, when my cautious fingers slid forwards to nestle in the soft underarm, and thence by slow degrees crept around in front to brush, to fondle, and finally to cup her proud right breast – the one farther from Cécile and away from me, next to Casilda. There my hand lay for a time, warmly ensconced, as though gloved in velvet, holding its treasured prize while Helen held her breath; and from that point of vantage, which stiffened under my palm, it sallied forth on brief excursions about her torso, pressing gently against the ribs, reconnoitering along the flank, delving down the smooth valley between her superbly hard, ripe, arrogant bubs, but returning home at intervals, beneath the loose folds of her scant Grecian tunic, to fasten with tender insistence on the alert, small nipple that stood up rigidly on guard, like a sentinel at his post.

Helen's quiet response, her admirable discretion and self-control, encouraged my inquisitive, errant fingers to probe her defences in search of a chink, a crack in the armour although even now, despite my keen enjoyment of a highly diverting situation, I was aware of its intrinsic dangers and conscious of my cruelty in subjecting my mistress's mistress to such a titillating trial of strength. Physically, so far as one could tell from her unruffled manner, she

132

appeared not to be suffering undue hardship; but her mental torment, I could only assume, must be acute enough in all conscience. Surely she was startled and embarrassed to get much livelier cooperation from me than she had bargained for; she had meant merely to lead me on a little, with a view of teasing Casilda, as it were, at second hand. I was to be given the blame for making a pass at her, but she counted on my not daring to go so far as to risk letting either Cécile or Lucien twig what I was up to – whereas Casilda, of course, would be quick to notice, since she was really the guilty party and therefore more vulnerably sensitive. Casilda evidently was spoiling for a fight, she was on the lookout for trouble. But it was Helen herself who was in trouble. I had turned the tables on her. My unexpectedly wholehearted entry into the spirit of the game spoiled everything. How was she going to deny indignantly, when taxed with it by Casilda after the show, that she had been responsible in any way for my scandalous behaviour? No doubt her line, as planned, was a sharp retort that would leave her girlfriend guessing. Casilda could then believe what she liked on the subject – and the worse the conclusions she reached, the better would Helen be pleased. Alas for the Baroness, she was the biter bit; I was proving rather more of a cad than she anticipated.

She was saved by the bell – that is, by the lights going up at the interval. Stoically she had maintained her poise during the past twenty minutes, keeping her eyes fixed on the stage, with her face turned slightly away from Cécile and screened to some extent by resting her left elbow on the ledge and her chin on her knuckles. It was a graceful pose that served a dual purpose in that the line of her cheek and shoulder, smothered in orchids, formed a blinker on one side to direct her daughter's innocent gaze towards the strutting singers below, while by bending forward from the hips she unobtrusively gave freer play to my caressing hand under the loosened folds of the bodice – if indeed so modest a term was applicable to the barely adequate top of her backless evening gown which plunged in a charmingly vacant V from her neck to her navel. Over wide areas of the trail my explorations had been conducted perforce without benefit of cover; to stray off the point for an instant was to venture heroically into the open. Now the first round ended with a burst of appluase; I dutifully withdrew my hand to join in the clapping.

'I enjoyed that immensely – didn't you?' I asked Helen.

She gave me a long searching stare, and shook her head slowly, dreamily, as though at a loss for words.

'I thought it divine, my dear Helen,' I insisted. 'Not a single false note – it really was quite remarkable. Not a sound that was discordant, not a quaver – from anyone.'

'Good God, Grey, what did you expect?' Lucien put in. 'A correct performance, naturally – faultless, above reproach, acceptable. But no great shakes –

nothing exciting. Don't listen to him, Cécile, he'll only mislead you.'

I laughed, and gazed steadily at Helen as we went outside to stretch our legs at the bar. 'Champagne for Cécile,' I ordered. 'And for what comes after. Have it your own way, *mon cher* Lucien – but I find this Aida wonderful, a complete revelation. She's my choice for the part from now on – the ideal slave-girl, docile, romantic, passionate and obedient: utterly enchanting. And such restraint! Amazing! You *feel* the latent power, the fiery temperament under that lovely outward calm . . . a grand performance. I don't know when I've enjoyed myself more, in some respects. The subtlety of it! Honestly, I can't wait for the finale . . . I'm dying to share her gallant death, the climax of her last panting sigh in her lover's arms.'

Helen's enigmatic look had not altered at all – unless it was not purely a mirage, that faint glint of a forgiving, secretive smile of connivance that I caught in her dark eyes. My own pleaded for a clear signal, but there was none to be had – which in itself I interpreted as a favourable sign. Encouragement would have been too much to ask. Still, she did say offhandedly:

'I'm so glad you're having a good time, Tony, at any rate. But one has to lose oneself entirely at the theatre, as I always tell Cécile. You miss the whole meaning and value of it if you allow anything to distract you, even for a moment. Every ounce of concentration is necessary to forget one's wordly cares. . . .'

135

'Distractions are Tony's chief aim in life,' Casilda cryptically announced. 'They are all he ever worries about.'

Helen made Cécile change places with her when we returned to the box, but I could not guess whether she hoped to keep me at arm's length this time or was effacing herself at the end of the row for greater privacy. The stratagem did not bother me, anyhow; I am ambidextrous. I drew my chair close up behind her, tilting it against the wall, so that I could keep watch on the others, while my left arm surreptitiously circled Helen's waist. I moulded her hip and explored her lap, spanning her belly and stroking her thigh. With a quick flick at my wrist, she tried to dislodge my hand, to push it away. Taken aback, I retired momentarily and then returned, with a definite gesture, to pursue my advance. Thrusting thumb and forefinger under her leg, just clear of the seat, I punished the flighty, wayward fool with a hefty pinch. That made her sit up all right; she jumped and let out a yelp that brought sharp inquiring looks from Cécile and Casilda, who peered at her suspiciously in the semidarkness.

'I've just remembered something.' Helen muttered lamely as an excuse.

I left her to simmer for a while – with excellent results. When I recommenced my stealthy encroachment along her left flank, the lesson had sunk in. She stayed quiet, and I could feel that she was braced in every nerve to undergo a further session of this enervating test, which troubled but assuredly did not displease her. She had allowed and induced me to take these liberties in the first place; now, it seemed to me, their effect on Casilda was no longer the whole object of the exercise, which she was beginning to assess, personally and directly, on its own merits. From every angle this was a most gratifying development; it was a highly flattering tribute to my talent for persuasion, a just reward attained by dint of subtle skill and patient effort. Nor was that all: to my delight I saw that I was killing two birds with one throw, for I became aware of a change of attitude in Casilda. I sensed this volte-face by instinct – there was little to convey it outwardly, save a vague air of greater friendliness on her part. I kept an eye on her, and smiled ingratiatingly when she turned her head, as she frequently did, to glance in our direction. I was operating in utter silence, of course, and the ample satin folds of Helen's dress covered and muffled my advance around her hip towards the promised land below the waist, but I could tell that Casilda had tumbled to what was going on. As soon as she made certain that her surmise was correct, though she could not follow my progress with any accuracy, it struck me that she was both relieved and amused to observe her friend's peculiar predicament. Cécile, at any rate, was safe, which apparently was the main consideration. Helen she must have regarded as fair game, for far from continuing to sulk; she now almost beamed on me. Things were looking up – though I could only conclude that the girl was plumb crazy.

Casilda's unfathomable motives at this point did not concern me. I had other good fresh fish to fry. It was a slow process, but I was doing nicely. The time came when, at a firm hint from me. Helen rose rapidly from her chair and rearranged her spreading skirts so that, to suit our mutual convenience, I was able to slip my open palm under her left buttock. There for a moment it lay imprisoned under the smooth, warm weight of her naked flesh – since she was stripped, beneath her heavy evening gown, for all emergencies – until I persuaded her to shift again, granting free passage between her legs to my probing fingers. At long last I had reached my goal, I could now caress her intimately, to my heart's content – and also, I hoped, to hers. Try as she might, she could not sit still: she was the dignified *grande dame* only down to the navel – below that, amid all the sumptuous decoration of the crowded theatre, the sparkling jewels and elegant bearing of the audience, the air filled with magnificent music, there was nothing but her open, eager, hot wet twat, a sensitive, sucking sea anemone hidden beneath the surface calm, yearning and squirming in answer to my touch, like some soft, warm furry beastie crouching in its moist, narrow trench under a thick pile of tangled leaves. True, every woman in the dimly lit auditorium guarded the same rich, scented female secret, nesting in repose between her cheeks on the padded seat, like a priceless heirloom set in a velvet case, to be produced and admired on special occasions. I agree, naturally, that the groove into which my fingers pried was one of many, in no way unique, not a particular or notable exception to the generous general rule of life. Or was it? Did it not differ in fact from all the rest in one respect, which was by far the most important? Of the myriad oysters in that vast oyster bed, young and old, fair or dark, pure and sweet or sick and rotten, did it not alone contain at this precise moment the fine, the incomparable, the only pearl of pleasure? There was none other in that shimmering swell, I'll warrant, that could boast of being at this very instant in the same condition. What single cunt in the whole collection could hold a candle now to Helen's? Her cup of happiness was well-nigh full to overflowing, as I played and toyed with it at will, rubbing, tickling, squeezing, coaxing the tender button that protruded from her parted lips, like a little pointed tongue, with delicate impudence, taunting as a flame, yet hard and anxious as a sentry's challenge at the gateway to a defenceless stronghold.

In the end I had to lift the siege, when the fortress was trembling on the brink of unconditional surrender. Helen's sexual excitement, bottled up inside the shapely urn of her cool, classical beauty, rose to a steaming degree of heat, almost on the bubble, like mulled resinous wine, as though about to splutter forth in a gurgle of sound from her dry throat, while the dwindling notes of the tragic duet from the condemned pair on the stage told us that Aida's strength, too, was ebbing away under the breathless strain of her martyrdom. It was a race between the four of us to see who would finish first, which couple – Verdi's *dramatis personae* or ourselves, so very much alive and nearly kicking – would consummate their fate before the other.

Harassed as she was, torn between the onrush of delight and her fear of discovery, desperate both from desire and with disappointment, Helen was denied all outlet for her feelings, which she could neither relieve nor restrain. Even if she had wanted to break off the engagement just as the culmination of her crisis seemed tantalisingly near there was nothing she could do about it, short of rising to her feet immediately, before the lights went up – an abrupt gesture which she dared not risk and did not trust herself to make without undue commotion. Besides, it was only a question of seconds. She hesitated, as well she might. Seated, her position placed her at my mercy. However tightly she strove to close her legs, she could not hope to dislodge my hand or protect the wide gap in her rearguard. By crushing her thighs together she might have warded off the boldest frontal attack; but I had broken through. I was already in full command of the situation, I had penetrated her bunker to its innermost depths, looting all that it had to offer, and her buttocks, outspread on the chair seat, were powerless now to bar my way or repulse my thrusting fingers, which held her fast on actual tenterhooks. . . .

Regretfully I was obliged to drop the unfinished business.

Lucien held forth so knowledgeably about this

rendering of *Aida* when the final curtain came down and we were wrapping ourselves up to face the damp outside world that I was seized with panic at the thought that, perhaps, he kept one eye open during a fair amount of the performance, after all. I convinced myself, however, that he was simply forestalling the sharp conjugal reprimand which such a lowbrow lapse on his part was liable to bring from the high-principled Helen. The joke, in fact, was on him. But anyway, to give the dirty old beast his due, would he be so uncivilised as to cut up rough if he had seen more than he ought of what had transpired between me and his stuck-up spouse, to whom clearly he was as much wedded as an ox to its yoke? He appeared tickled pink – probably, with the show over, at the prospect of getting off quickly to bed. At any rate he would not hear of going on somewhere for supper. Helen assured everyone that I must be famished – but of course Cécile would have to bundle home at once, she had an early start to make on the morrow and, as they had been in the country all day, she hadn't even packed. Poor Cécile! Her eager acceptance of my invitation, when I suggested I be allowed to escort the three ladies to a nightclub, was firmly quashed by her mother, whose nerves were evidently on edge.

Not only was the Baroness extremely agitated but it struck me that she was more than a trifle tipsy. She chattered like a magpie most of the way, as I drove them all back in the car to Regent's Park, but at times fell into deep, dreamy silences which she would break with a sudden fresh spate of verbosity, quite out of context. She made no move to join us on their doorstep when we arrived and Lucien asked me in for a nightcap, so I was grateful to Casilda for taking charge of the situation at once with natural ease and diplomacy: she kissed Cécile good-bye 'in case I don't see you again in the morning' and told Lucien 'I suppose I must help Helen toy with the expensive supper Tony seems set on buying us – *à demain* then, and thank you for a most enjoyable evening.'

'You don't mind if I join you?' she inquired as we went back to the car. I shook my head.

'Of course not. But I'm going to lure Helen straight to my place if I can. Don't interfere.'

'Whatever for? Hadn't I better make myself scarce then? You don't want me there.'

'I do indeed. And Helen may, anyhow. I suspect it's you she's after, really. We shall see. . . .'

'Well I'll be damned!' Casilda laughed. 'Okay, try your luck,' she added, climbing in beside me.

'Wouldn't it be a good idea to skip the stuffy *boîte* and go back home with you, Tony?' she asked, as we started down Baker Street. 'Helen, what do you think? Personally I could do with a bit of a rest from crowds and music. . . .'

'I wanted to talk to Tony,' Helen objected, 'and I thought at a nightclub – '

'My God, yes – impossible,' Casilda cut in, deliberately misunderstanding her. 'Too distracting – all the wrong atmosphere. I couldn't agree more.'

'But isn't he ravenous? He must get something to eat,' Helen argued.

'Oh, there's plenty of food in the house. I'll fix us up something, don't worry.' Casilda's tone was bland, friendly, and definite. We veered towards Chelsea.

'Suits me,' I said. 'I have a little caviar up my sleeve. How about that? And a magnum of Mumm. You've never been there, have you, Helen? I'd like you to see my humble abode.'

'I'm sure I shall enjoy your pictures,' Helen replied, but the inflection of her voice gave me no clue whether she was being polite or ironical. Did she mean me to infer that she was proof against so transparent a subterfuge, or that we must resign ourselves to Casilda's tiresome intrusion? What was in her mind? She seemed puzzled, in a fuddled way, that our chaperon should know so much about my domestic arrangements. Had she really only wanted to be alone with me for a cosy *tête-à-tête* over dinner in a discreet, ill-lit corner of some classy dive? To discuss Casilda perhaps? Vain I may be at times (as which of us isn't, in such matters?) yet even so I hesitated to believe, on the strength of our recent slap-and-tickle, that she was all set to go through with it and aching to tuck up with me right away. I was perfectly prepared to take pity on her, since I had worked her up to this lecherous pitch – but what came next must remain to be seen. We had sauntered off down a side alley, the adventure was on a new tack . . . let her take the helm for a bit. I had every excuse to indulge my

143

male conceit. I might have claimed a just dividend. If the lesbian leopard had changed its spots, and was starting to purr, whose doing was that? It was I, not Casilda, whom she should call upon to quench the fire which my sympathetic intervention had so charitably kindled for her in the weeds of her deserted back-garden. For my part, however, I was determined to proceed with caution, modesty and candour. I preferred to discount the glow of alcoholic optimism and not to rush things, but wait for the clear green light. So far, so good. A most entertaining party might develop, with the pair of them in tow. But neither Cassy nor I must rub Helen up the wrong way or bungle it at all. She was in heat and in her randy condition could go sour on us as easy as winking, for I still thought it was Casilda she craved at this point – Casilda, who had been so standoffish of late, and whom she probably aimed to win back tonight, come what may, at any cost, under my roof if necessary . . . in a mood of sensual, sentimental intoxication – not unlike my own – she was ready, I felt, to risk a showdown with her loved one which was unthinkable at home in her own house, where Lucien or Cécile would hear them if she staged a flaming row, or maybe, too, if it went well and a passionate, tiddly reconciliation took place. . . .

On the other hand it hadn't been her idea certainly that Casilda should join us, nor had she exactly jumped for joy at the prospect of our all whisking out to Chelsea. What possible hope was there of fun and games with me, though, since we were not alone and hadn't a chance to get rid of the tactless Casilda? Most likely she could not have said herself what she desired so intensely, with such deep, troubled longing in her crotch that she shut her eyes to nurse the turmoil and the ache inside her. . . .

Anyhow, here was my lemon-yellow door; we had arrived.

CHAPTER SEVEN

Now Helen was lucky: fate played right into her lap. No sooner had we crossed the threshold than Casilda announced, decisively, that she would take over the commissariat and did not wish to have anyone else barging into the kitchen. 'I know where everything is,' she said. 'Just tell me what it's to be – bacon and eggs or cold chicken with salad?'

'Both, darling,' I answered, but Helen asked for 'only the caviar, please, if I may.'

Leaning against the mantlepiece she watched me uncork and ice the champagne, but almost before the menial duty was done she had melted into my arms. With hers about my neck, reaching upwards on her toes, she clung to my mouth in a burning, greedy kiss that seemed to have no end, until my roving hands had almost had their fill of feeling firm flesh under the slithering, soft satin of her dress

146

– a subtle, exquisitely thrilling contrast of textures and temperatures, between cold and warm, crinkly and smooth, limp and solid, yet both combined, her naked body with its sumptuously sleek covering, the single source of mixed and most marvellous tactile sensations. Eventually, without dissolving our joined lips, I put off the yoke of her giddy embrace and tenderly unwrapped this alabaster statue from its protective folds, which I unfastened and removed, disclosing its ideal purity of form, as one would eagerly but cautiously extract a Ming vase out of a straw and paper parcel. First I unpinned the clump of orchids – and the contamination of their over-ornate, sickly exoticism – from a crevasse between bare shoulder and boiled shirt; then off came the long, plain, full expensive garment, from which she nimbly stepped, as though escaping through its deep, vermillion ring of fire on the floor about her feet, while I, released at last, knelt and took off her tiny, high-heeled shoes.

Once more, as she stood in the light of the blazing new logs, my hands ran over every inch of this slim little Aphrodite, whose bosom was there, staring me in the face, at point-blank range a prey to my lips, which absorbed the stiff defiance of its twin gun turrets, smothering any faint signs of a token resistance that might still be met elsewhere on a wide front. Here was an opportunity denied to me, naturally, at the threatre. I was following the logical, correct, classic sequence, progressing along the regular route from one erotic zone to the next, well-nigh automatically, for there is nothing

in the world that varies so little, yet is always so
novel, so freshly inspiring, as this same old unalter-
able strategy of the senses, which is particularly
delightful on the very account of its unfailing
simplicity, that miraculous blessing born anew in
each case from primordial instinct, universal
experience, mutual agreement and constant practice. I moulded her breasts, her hips, her navel,
buttocks, thighs and mount of Venus with my
palms and thumbs as a sculptor would shape the
planes and masses of cold clay to recreate the
beauty of his model – but it was not from the life
that I worked out Helen's figure; the reality, the
palpitating splendour of life itself was the divine
material that, on my knees as though praying, I
now held and pressed ecstatically in my hands.

Her body, magnificently a woman's, was as light
as a child's. Rising to my feet, I lifted her off hers,
carried her to the sofa and laid her down on it like
a doll. But half the charm of a doll is its fancy frills,
whereas Helen's reclining pale nudity among the
cushions lent her the appearance of a cut flower
herself – like one of those wicked, waxen-white
blooms of her corsage which I ostentatiously shut
away in a drawer as a keepsake, before returning
to carry on where I had left off: bending down
again, in other words, to dally with her dear wee
tits, which I nibbled, sucked and nuzzled for a
while until I judged the moment had come to lower
my sights and dive more deeply into the dark,
narrow, salty creek between her sheltering
thighs . . . ah, the cool, chic, imperturbable hostess

Helen, with her lofty airs of intellectual superiority, her overweening culture and meticulous judgements, where was all that snobbish highfalutin nonsense now? Here we had the same good old, useful bag of tricks as ever, opened up for inspection at the customs, under my prying nose. What had she got to declare? Her rare spiritual values? Her precious taste? Nothing exceptional about this paraphernalia; it was just as one expected it would be – familiar enough, yet somehow easier to recall than to define from memory, its precise flavour pungent but swift to dissolve, fading upon the tongue. No luxury at any rate, but quite the reverse – by far the most ordinary, least costly of perfumes, not dutiable and (maybe for this reason also) that which many men prefer.

I had seen Helen in these straits before, though she was not aware of it. Nevertheless, her total transformation came as an enchanting shock to me. The difference between watching and doing, of course, was incalculable: I was most actively involved in the transports that now sent shivers vibrating through Helen's fragile frame; I held her in my power, I was responsible for what was happening to her, for the destruction of her poise, her fainting condition, her loss of any semblance of serenity in a dizzy swirl of desire which I stirred with every ounce of skill and energy that I could muster. Absorbed by my task of demolition, I proceeded steadily to undermine her façade, and all that mattered to either of us at this juncture was my mastery over her emotions. We were both, I think, quite oblivious of our surroundings. I did not care if Casilda were suddenly to appear from the kitchen with our supper, which Helen no doubt had utterly forgotten – or she may have imagined that it would be served properly, in formal fashion, elsewhere. How could the Baroness conceive that I seldom make use of the dining room next door, except to show pictures in the best light? Her body was brimful and oozing with sensuality, her brain was emptied of coherent thought. At times a low groan escaped through her contorted lips, but for the most part she seemed bereft of speech and only gasped occasionally: 'Aah, it's so good . . . so good . . .'

For her, this was wild enthusiasm. She was all over me, you might say, in more senses than one. We had no time to spare, and indeed it was ripe, as I could tell, for immediate action. Further preliminaries were obviously unwanted and unnecessary. The goose had been plucked and cooked in readiness for the feast. It was clear that my guest required to be served soon without delay. Even the most finicky operator could have found no excuse to procrastinate any longer. She had slid down flat on her back on the sofa, raising her knees in evident anticipation of open warfare. Zero hour had struck. It only remained for me to go over the top, the invasion was planned, I was to carry the day with fire and the sword.

I sprang up and whipped my weapon from its sheath – my alas not-so-trusty blade, which this time appeared swollen with confidence, like its

owner, as it stood at the salute with the proud,
menacing mien of the hardened duelist who has
laid many an adversary full length upon the field
of honour. But Helen showed no interest in the
sight whatsoever. Her eyes were shut, her head
turned away. I was a trifle chagrined, I confess, by
her abstracted air, her inattention to the point I
wished to put to her, clinching our long and heated
argument. After all, in the nature of things she
could not have been offered such weighty, ocular
proof of male devotion for a number of years now.
You'd have thought it must be a matter of relative
importance to her at least; normally it is not a
question that any of her sex can regard with
complete indifference.

Still, there it was. Let her have it her own way.
She was eaten up with impatience, for all that.
And I could not afford to wait about, we hadn't a
moment to spare – not even for me to shed the
encumbrance of my stiff shirt, white tie and tails.
I propped her trim little rump on to a fat cushion,
and gave her what she had coming to her with a
straight, strenuous uppercut that took the slack out
of her rigging. Ha'ah, yes – there, that brought her
round, snap back to life, as though touched, tapped,
struck by a magic wand! Up came her face, open-
mouthed, with staring eyes, startled and frowning
in an anguish of delight below me, as I raised
myself on my arms, pressing her shoulders down
hard into the soft, deep mound of cushions on the
sofa. She was with me now, and no mistake. At the
first flick of the conductor's baton, the music

crashed out, the orchestra blared, *vivace*, *bravo*, *fortissimo*! Away we went, at breakneck speed, like the wind blowing a full gale – on, on! – for all we were jolly well worth, racing ahead in double time together.

But it went wrong, the excitement petered out – I couldn't tell you why. It was one of those things . . . we were doing fine – but after that flying start, the sweet, ineffable fervour of the first few moments which, packed with the wonder of rediscovery, are the best of all, the best for both, the most divine because, paradoxically, the climax, better yet, is still to come . . . gradually, imperceptibly we began to droop, to wilt, the flame commenced to dwindle, slowly to sink, unaccountably we lost our grip . . . there was no outward sign of failure that anyone watching could have detected, I feel sure – and maybe it was not Helen's fault nor was it mine; that much I know. Yet our eager illusions were dashed, the promise of an imminent mutual cataclysm was denied, our dazzling inward glimpse of paradise faded like a mirage . . .

I gritted my teeth and strained every nerve, but pleasure gave place to resentment as I laboured on, getting nowhere. It was a bad dream . . . I had leaped into the saddle and galloped off into the night, since we must flee to safety in a distant land, my willing mare and I – dear life depended on it – yet, spur her as I would, the rolling, endless desert sands refused to move beneath her pounding hooves, which shook the earth with ever more desperate and jerky strides, exhaustion claimed us

both, as I lay prostrate across the pommel, and
her staggering gait hammered into my mind the
dreadful realisation that there was no escape, dawn
would not break on these eternal wastes. How well
I knew the galling misery of such defeats! I loathed
the thought of letting Helen down – but with the
best will in the world I could not entirely absolve
her from her share of the blame. I had embarked
on this inconclusive struggle radiant with hope and
bursting with desire. Here I was, caught in a trap
of chugging drudgery – but if we were both
deluded, why should she have more right than I to
complain of frustration? There had been no collapse
as yet on my part: my member was still on the job,
hard at it, although his original zeal had diminished
somewhat now, as was only natural. He had done
manful work, in all conscience, and it would be
maligning him to describe his present effort as half-
hearted. I was giving her the regulation six inches,
confound it, and as many twists and turns as she
was entitled to expect at her age. Most likely we
had had too much to drink, she and I – that might
well be the answer. At least it explained the debacle
in my case, I was convinced. The symptoms were
recognisable, leaving little room for doubt . . . but
could she make the same excuse? Any full-blooded,
normal woman would have come by now, releasing
me from the wearisome obligation of expending my
remaining strength on this futile enterprise. I had
sworn to myself that I would ring the bell with this
damned, lecherous lesbian bitch before giving in, if
I died in the attempt. But it was not to be. What

ignominy, that she should cheat me twice over, robbing me of both my orgasm and hers! Not that I could accuse her of failing to meet me more than half-way. Her timing, the movements of her pelvis and the shifts of her whole body, her muscular contractions, lascivious ingenuity and vigour in response to my dull thrusts were a credit, frankly, to one so frail and so long out of practice in the act of coitus. We clung together with dogged determination to squeeze the final, assuaging spasm from our agonised embrace – it seemed so near – when suddenly Casilda entered and crossed the room with a loaded tray, which she set down on the table next door, merely glancing at our entangled mass on the sofa as she passed.

'Don't mind me, you two – carry on,' she remarked in a casual, quiet tone of voice. 'Supper isn't quite ready yet.'

Stopping as though shot, Helen let out a little shriek of shame and embarrassment. She flung an arm across her face to hide its expression of pathetic misery, not realising that as she lay beneath me, almost obliterated, it was shielded from Casilda' view by my black-coated shoulder.

Casilda's attitude, on the other hand, evinced merely amiable and sympathetic curiosity. She emerged from the dining room, gnawing a chicken's leg, and hovered behind the sofa for a moment or two, reflectively biting shreds of meat off the bone as she observed our antics – or rather mine – with as much interest as the school coach takes in a training bout between a couple of fifth-form boxers.

'Hold it a minute,' she advised with unconscious irony, which I mistook for heavy sarcasm. 'Don't come yet, either of you – I'll be back in one second.'

The instant she was out of the room, Helen, who had been lying flat and still under me, like a corpse, began struggling wildly, trying to break away.

'Quick, quick – get off me, let me go, please, Tony, get off, let me go!' she clamoured, pushing at my chest and at my chin in a violent, vain endeavour to lift my oppressive weight.

She had gone crazy. What? Stop now? When Casilda was taking it so well? She must be out of her mind. On me Casilda's entry had produced exactly the opposite effect – it had immediately revived my flagging spirits and administered a sharp stimulant to my lost appetite, which brightened under her scrutiny like a rusty old lamp polished anew: Aladdin's lamp, no less, whose genie at a twinkle sprang to life in Helen's guts, prepared to do my bidding. I was another man now, armed with redoubled courage. I started in at once to rodger that silly, grizzling fool as furiously as an angry rooster treads a cackling hen.

Nevertheless, it did no good. I gripped Helen by the buttocks, pulling them fiercely down and apart in each hand, to nail and stretch the slit for deeper penetration, while bracing my feet against the arm of the sofa; but I could strike no answering spark in her. She was not even hostile – simply inert. This lack of antagonism was worse than any mere absence of cooperation. My fresh spurt waned. Resuscitation had been momentary, as briefly invigorating as a pinch of snuff up the nostrils. By the time Casilda returned from the kitchen and poured the champagne, I had run down like a clock. The game was up, psychologically doomed. I gave in, and withdrew.

I sat back, clasping my forehead. Casilda held out glasses to each of us, but Helen had rolled over on her side. She buried her face in the cushions, and her shoulders shook. There was no sound in the room, though she was sobbing.

Casilda looked from one to the other of us with a puzzled, inquiring smile.

'A drawn match,' I told her. 'Even after extra time.'

'Really?' Casilda laughed. 'You don't mean it! Helen, I'm surprised at you,' she said.

During the long pause that followed, Casilda warmed herself by the fire. Helen had not touched the glass on the floor beside her. She did not speak. I wondered if she had fallen asleep from exhaustion, both bodily and emotional. Casilda appeared lost in thought.

'Supper is ready, you know,' she announced. There were no takers.

She shrugged, and stared with amusement at the pair of us, but when she came over and sat next to me, away from Helen, who lay curled up in a ball, it was with a comically reluctant gesture, as of one bestowing alms on a beggar. Pressing her lips to mine, she settled herself comfortably and treated me to a long, voluptuous searching kiss that sent hot shivers down my spine, while her hand dragged my battered tool once more out of my fly into the limelight, and frigged it firmly, expertly, with her long, slow, gentle strokes, at the same time subtly massaging my flaccid nuts, until in a short while I had a horn on me that any sultan might have envied.

Stars danced before my eyes as, head back, gagged by her darting tongue, I relaxed – except at the focal point – in surrender to her skilled manipulations, which vaguely I sought to repay in kind with groping fingers. She allowed my hand to reach its goal, accepting its somewhat automatic tribute to her sex with proper and ladylike complaisance; but when my other hand strayed to the neck of her Prussian-blue taffeta evening gown, she pushed it away and nodded in Helen's direction. I obeyed the order – only to have Helen sit up like a jack-in-the-box the moment I slid a caressing palm between her thighs.

'Don't touch me!' she almost screamed.

We gazed at her in astonishment.

'Helen – for heaven's sake, what's come over you?' I expostulated.

She did not look at me. Glaring murderously at Casilda, she cowered at the end of the sofa, trembling from head to foot, as though fighting to find words in some dark inner whirlpool of rage.

'Casilda,' she pronounced at last, in a voice colder than a mortuary slab: 'This man is your lover. You have been lying to me. Your life with me was a lie. Oh, my God, the whole situation is too repulsive, too loathsome! You have hurt me terribly. I did not deserve this of you. I shall never recover from your deceit. I will leave you now – with him. I am going home.'

'There, there, Helen darling,' Casilda said. 'Calm down, now, take it easy. We've shared so many secrets in the past . . . look, this isn't a secret. It's just exactly what you need. You're a tiny bit hysterical, my sweet. Don't be so rude to Tony. He can't stand up for himself. But he's all right now. I fixed it for you. Come on, honey – let him give you a damn good lay. It won't go wrong this time. Listen. I'll go out of the room, if you'd rather . . .'

I thought Helen would fly at her. She leaned forward, hugging herself, taut as a coiled spring. She was a porcupine, a miniature atomic rocket. There was a mad, homicidal glint in her eyes.

'I'm going home,' she repeated. 'Where's my wrap? Let me out of here.'

Casilda only laughed. 'Well you're missing a swell opportunity,' she said. 'It's a lot better, this, than that beastly old dildo of yours – take my word for it. Don't be so stupid, Helen. You're wasting all my beautiful handiwork. Go on, Tony – fuck her, why don't you? What are you waiting for? She doesn't know what she wants. That's what's the matter with her, poor poppet. She can have *me* any time. But one does like a little variety . . .'

I turned towards the blazing bare bundle of outraged womanhood, as she backed away on the sofa, with some trepidation. It was an exciting idea, all the same. I was attracted and frightened. If only Casilda would help, maybe . . . You would have to get someone to hold her down — at any rate for a start. It would be like taking liberties with a small black panther.

'Helen,' I pleaded. 'You really can't leave me in this state, you know. Don't go home yet — stick around. I've shown already how much I wanted you — and I still do. It was wonderful, Helen — you are quite marvellous. Such a lovely, lovely body . . . but first let me get all these hampering clothes off. I'll take you home later, both of you.'

At one bound, before I could lay a finger on her — I approached rather gingerly — she was across the room and had squatted down facing us, in front of the fire. She snatched up her dress from a chair, where Casilda had placed it, and tucked its vermillion folds modestly about her knees. Casilda bubbled with mirth like a fountain.

'A ladybug to the life,' she said. 'And, oh dear, what an awful rebuff! Must you fly away?'

She still held my cock in her hand; even when she shoved me over towards Helen she had not relinquished it. Now, in full view of our audience, she bent down and stiffened my prick again to her liking with a few careful kisses. So far as I was concerned, she could have gone on forever, licking and tickling the tip of it with her tongue — but apparently she had other plans. For the second time that night my phallus was enveloped in a narrow, hot, tender prison that kept it for a while confined and captive. Which fleshly dungeon was the happier burial place — Casilda's mouth or Helen's nice tight twat? Before I could decide that delicate point, she set him free, jumped to her feet, and standing over me, with her back turned on Helen, she picked up the hem of her dress and pulled it over her hips, where with both hands she rolled it in a bunch about her waist. It was a lewd and slightly ludicrous figure she cut, towering above me on her high heels and long, straight legs, so temptingly naked all the way up, except for a simple black lace triangle, like a bull's-eye, that merely added provocation to the ensemble, but with the top half of the body more than decently covered – too much, too grandly clad, hindered and overdecked in an accumulation of glistening taffeta and jewels. It was a lovely sight, as festive, touching, brilliant as a Christmas tree. I studied it in detail gladly, with leisurely appreciation, and gently tugging the dainty patch of her lace down to her ankles, unmasked the gorgeous thicket of brown curls that sprouted out at me, demanding my instant homage, at eye level.

'No, that's enough – hurry, lean back!' Casilda said.

Not till then, as she stepped forward, straddling my legs with her fork widely separated, and lowered herself without haste onto the turgid prong which I guided and aimed into the open slot that softly descended to close down upon it, to meet its match, its fitting mate, the richest gift from heaven, was I suddenly chilled by the alarming thought of Helen's ferocious jealousy. From where she sat, huddled near the fire, she must have witnessed the whole operation from just that low angle that was calculated to spare her nothing. I could picture what she saw – the gaping rear view under Casilda's outthrust tail, as it hung suspended in midair, with the tangled tuft parted by her spreading thighs to show the scarlet gash of her vagina that slowly swallowed up my penis inch by inch and dropped to rest in contact with my scrotum, sealing it across the entrance to the pit, as with a boulder to stop a secret passage. And this was all only the beginning of the film – suppose the spectacle proved more than she could bear? The sequel, with Casilda riding a cock-horse hell for leather, might end disastrously. What could I do, in my helpless position, if Helen were to attack her girl friend from behind? At one blow – with the poker, for instance – she could kill her. I would be lucky indeed if they only scratched their eyes out. Was I to sit back and let these two harpies fight over me? A gentleman was bound to intervene. Brawling was one thing; insults did no lasting harm. But at all costs I must avoid bloodshed on the premises ... Casilda was the stronger, no doubt – but we were at a frightful disadvantage. The spectre of imminent murder loomed over me in the rocking, plunging, writhing shape of the victim as, swaying to and fro, and tossing her mane – though I was the mount and she the rider – Casilda bore down on top of me until, our roles reversed, with all her weight on my belly, she seemed to be screwing us further and further into each other ...

With head thrown back – an easy target – while clutching the crumpled dress across her tits, she was as bare as Godiva around the middle, whereas Helen now, I could see, had got her clothes on. Peering anxiously under a sawing elbow, I kept an eye on her to prevent any surprise move . . . she was making ready, as I guessed, for a quick getaway after the deed. There was no means of defence within my reach, not even the bottle. Helen had collected all her things . . . I spoke to her urgently. I begged her to stay, to have a drink, or a bite to eat. I promised again to take her home – if she could wait just a moment . . . I offered her coffee – there was some in the kitchen, I said.

She did not deign to reply. She found the orchids and threw them into the fire. Then, with her face averted, she delivered herself of a valedictory address to Casilda, who took no notice. It was a curt and definite farewell, but not particularly abusive. She would never consent to see the immoral, faithless slut again so long as she lived. She ran to the door, and was gone.

We came, I recall, as she went.

CHAPTER EIGHT

Calm reigned over the cabbage patch. Now that we had each other to ourselves, with Helen out of the way, I presume some sentiment oddly akin to love must have accounted for the agreeable fact that our life together showed no signs of palling on either of us, although in every respect save one – except in the eyes of the law, that is – we were as bad as married. I never could have guessed that I might take to a virtual state of wedlock so meekly, with such benign resignation and tolerance. Casilda fetched her belongings next day from Regent's Park, timing the visit so as to avoid her former hostess of many years, who would be seeing Cécile off at the airport, and immediately took up residence with me. My spare room was certainly not large enough to billet a lady in the style to which Casilda was accustomed, but by unpacking only about a third of her wardrobe and stowing a dozen pieces of luggage in the basement she was able to settle in fairly comfortably as my guest for a couple of months or so. That, I believe, was what I suggested. Casilda put it differently: 'for the duration,' she said. I liked the arrangement: it suited me to a T, and the problem of how to get rid of her eventually, when I'd had enough of a good thing and my bachelor character reasserted itself, was a bridge I felt I could cross when we came to it.

The charm of the situation, its saving grace, was that we were free to play at matrimony in make-believe, like children keeping house, and the kick we got from this perverse parlour game was due to the knowledge that our honeymoon romp would entail no dreary aftermath of domesticity, deception, debt or doubts. The great final bust-up with Helen had cleared the air, and our predominantly sexual liaison took on a new lease of life, since we no longer suffered the constraints attached to what is generally – and graphically – described as a hole-in-the-corner affair. Indeed we now went to the other extreme, seldom caring to be parted from one another, but neglecting our many friends entirely, once we had set up a home. If two such socially minded types as ourselves did not consider this abstention any sacrifice, but found adequate companionship in their own company, then, as somebody remarked about us wryly, 'it must cover a multitude of sins.' True, we spent long hours in bed together – withdrawn into our private shell, if you like – but most of that time we slept. Sensual delight had not gone stale on us already, after a few short weeks; it was scored to a slower, easier beat. The conjugal state, however temporary and really blissful, takes every couple that way, by an immutable decree of nature. The swiftest racer goes farthest if he sometimes rests on his oar.

Casilda denied indignantly that she might miss the habit of her homosexual gambols with Helen, and I was content to have exchanged a measure of variety and freedom for a unique asset in the regular services of the only female of my acquaintance who never failed to ring the bell with me. We were, quite simply, in clover.

It was at an exhibition of paintings by a young Austrian artist, one wintry February evening, that we ran into Janet, whom Casilda had not met before, though I, needless to say, had related to her many memorable incidents from the annals of our tempestuous, jaunty-blithe, dingdong engagement, which had lasted on and off for nearly seven years and broke up in final disorder, to our immense mutual relief, on the way in her car to the registry. I have a weak ankle still as a result of that thousand-and-first fracas, while Janet wears two wedding rings, a false front tooth, and a big white streak in her dark mane as reminders of what she calls 'the pubic wars' or 'my grim Grey period.' We were now fond friends, sharing the curious jocular charm that passions spent acquire as a patina with age, but I had not seen her, either, nor her inoffensive Scottish husband, Andrew, since 'the evening you vamoosed halfway through dinner,' as Janet reminded me rather tartly. She shrugged off my apologies. 'I only hope she was worth it,' she said, 'I assume so, as we haven't heard from you since.'

We were standing under the shadows of an elongated Battersea Bridge at sunset, and Casilda drifted in from the next room at that moment, catalogue in hand, looking for me.

'I rather like that,' Janet declared, waving a glove at some bathers on a canal bank and narrowly missing Casilda's nose as she approached.

'Me too,' I said. I introduced them. 'This was the reason why I owe you and Andrew an especially good dinner.' I explained, 'to make up, Janet dear, for my rudeness in leaving you that night a trifle abruptly.'

'Janet, the famous Janet!' Casilda exclaimed. 'Knowing Tony as we do, I needn't tell you how often he drags your name into the conversation. It's a household word with us, if you'll forgive me saying so.'

'Oh, my God, yes, I'm sorry for you,' Janet laughed. 'He's such a tireless reminiscer, isn't he? You must know all – but everything – about me in the most lurid detail, I'm sure. How dismal of you, Tony!'

'Let me give you the lowdown on Casilda in return,' I offered. 'When can you have a quiet, gossipy lunch with me?'

'I insist on getting my word in first,' Casilda stated. 'We girls have a lot in common. What do

166

you say, Janet? Unless we let him come along as well – just to eat, shut up, and listen.'

We took a stroll round the gallery, discussing Klaus Ritter's quite commendable stuff, and gave Janet a few drinks at the pub on the corner before she dived into the Underground for Hampstead, where we were to dine with them the following Thursday. My two darlings, past and present, had taken to each other in a big way, and I was completely ignored in the frowzy saloon bar while they got on like a row of houses on fire, chattering and giggling so gaily that I noticed several staid customers regarding them with greater interest and more frankly amused admiration than any freak or foreigner can normally count on arousing among the British at home. They made a striking pair of beauties, even for the West End, I will admit, in that dowdy setting, though there was nothing bizarre about Janet's lean English looks and Casilda was so un-American an expatriate that she could happily refer to herself as a crossbred mongrel, instead of just taking it for granted.

'I'm nuts about that Janet of yours,' Casilda informed me as the station swallowed my ex-fiancée down its fetid gullet. 'She's loads of fun – and madly attractive, in a famished style of looks. Not much of her, is there?'

'If Janet were ever to shed an ounce of weight off her spare frame, skinny would be the only word for her. But that isn't feasible because there ain't no flesh on her anywhere that she could lose, as I used to tell her, without the light showing through.

You'd have to scoop to hollow out even a sliver of Janet. My cronies used to describe her as scrawny, but dressmakers call it 'slenderly built.' She's a sylph – irremediably thin, or, as she says herself, 'thin with knobs on.' That's more accurate. The knobs are all there, and the curves – long and slight and sinewy as a greyhound's, but perfectly in proportion and finely drawn, like a streamlined, sensitive piece of machinery, a shiny steel instrument of some sort. Janet, stripped, presents a far less gaunt appearance than the fashionable self you saw in her clothes. A bit lanky, of course, but a damned sight more human in shape when she's naked.'

'So I would imagine,' Casilda commented with a smile. 'You and your nudes! You analyse and compare every woman's body you come across. Wouldn't you do better to photograph us all for the record, instead of trying to remember a whole jumbled mass of mental notes?'

Where Janet was concerned, if I wished to be critical, I would set against her undoubted good points two anatomical flaws that are often found in this tall breed of Englishwomen. Her tits were appealing, firm and excellent, although of course too small – but they also were placed too low and rather too far apart, pointing outwards, which gave her a flat chest at first sight, and yet, almost as a pleasant afterthought, a distinctly feminine bosom. This was charming enough in itself, once discovered; but it seemed to have little, if any, connection with the strongly marked, splendid pectoral muscles that could scarcely be needed to lift those sweet, prancing, miniature breasts. Secondly, under her fork, at the top of her long, lean shanks, though she was not bow-legged, there was an empty space, an unsightly, inverted triangular gap between the thighs, which were devoid of any fat, so that, here, at the vital intersection itself, you got more room for manoeuvre than is usually provided for a man's comfort or the woman's ease in accommodating a visitor's retinue, however bulky. It always struck me that this fault – I would hardly call it a drawback – detracted from the obvious merits of Janet's smooth, pretty concave belly and proud, very prominent mount of Venus, which were among her best features, to my taste.

The Mackenzies lived on the far side of Hampstead. Andrew wore glasses, an incipient paunch, and a canny, good-natured expression, as though all three attributes were as congenial to him as the pink complexion which was a shade darker, if anything, than his now greying carroty hair. Physically he was not prepossessing, but he had the proverbial Scottish traits of dry humour and reserved gravity, though he carried neither to that excess which amounts, in many of his race, to unwarranted conceit and taciturn boorishness. The martinis, after a hard day's work at his printing office, loosened his tongue before we sat down to the delicious, unorthodox sort of meal in which both our host, and hostess, as butler and cook, were right to take great pride, for its succession of exotic

169

specialities was typical of the house. Casilda could not conceal her admiring envy and thereby won Andrew's heart, so that no stranger joining us at table would have been able to guess who among the assembled company were intimate friends or had never met before in their lives.

Andrew assured me, when I complimented him on the choice variety of his food and wines, that above all else he had a passion for his trade as a typographer, which took up every moment of his time, he said, apart from weekend golf, because he had allowed it to become his hobby as well. He too was a collector – of books. 'I have a very small library,' he told me, 'but most of the items in it are prize specimens, and some are unique. You'll see – though they may not be much up your street. I only go in for fine bindings and perfect examples of print.'

Andrew kept his cigars also in the cosy little room off the hall, where we retreated with a decanter and plenty of coffee to inspect the shelves that glowed, like a tapestry, with rich tones of leather and gilt. He showed me a wealth of magnificent volumes, among them half a dozen that I had not merely seen before in booksellers' lists or behind glass, and though I did not doubt his word it occurred to me that sometimes perhaps he let the merits of subject matter outweigh the intrinsic value of the production. There was a priceless Aretion, the *Decameron*, Crebillon's *Sofa* and other curious works that may have owed their presence there to outward beauty, but, rubbing shoulders with them, I found a tome or two – a smudgy, tattered copy of Rochester's *Sodom*, for example – whose rarity alone would rate them worthy of inclusion, whereas the few modern editions, maybe a score, in a separate section, belonged to the same single class of illustrated masterpieces intended solely for perusal by adult and discriminating readers.

I was pouring over the pages of Sade's *Justine* when the telephone pealed out beside me, and the bookworm Andrew answered it. An agitated voice spluttered at length into his ear, eliciting no more than an occasional gruff query or dour affirmative in reply. Finally he snapped: 'Well, all right then – I'll have to go down and cope with it myself, I shan't be long.'

He turned to me. 'I'm sorry,' he said. 'A call from that fool of a head printer. Apologise to the girls on my behalf. I might get back, with luck, before you go.'

He started to ring for a taxi, but I insisted on driving him at least as far as the station. It was a dirty night, and I was glad to let myself into the warmth with his latchkey. *En passant* I picked up another cigar and some brandy from the study before joining the ladies.

There they were, on the sofa together, in front of the drawing-room fire, but I could not say that I caught them in a compromising situation, because they showed no sign of heeding my intrusion in the least. Janet was almost lost to view in Casilda's arms, but both were still fully clothed. Casilda was

kissing and fondling my former love, who very
evidently relished her attentions, for her head was
thrown back, her eyes were shut, and she was
sighing and squirming in that abandoned way she
had, which I remembered so well. This went on for
some time, until Casilda, becoming aware of my
diffident presence, looked up and gave me a wink
of the most entrancing vulgarity. If she did not
wave in recognition, it was because both her hands
were deeply engaged, at first on a roving mission
and then in a definite pincer movement that
appeared to rouse our hostess from uneasy slumbers
to a vocal and increasingly active share in the
proceedings. Janet's staring peepers opened like a
doll's, she suddenly found a great deal to say – all
of it highly flattering to her newly acquired friend
– and her arms, linked about Casilda's neck,
dragged the happy, wide, scarlet mouth down to
her own, silencing them both, to some extent, for
neither one of the excited pair could speak again
for a while in coherent terms, though the language
they used was an expressive universal *lingua franca*
sound beyond the limits of speech, as they kissed,
mumbled, panted, gasped and sighed. . . .

I was sitting back in a large armchair, quietly
puffing at my mellow Larriñaga, as utterly at ease
as a millionaire impresario watching a deliriously
popular stage turn from the wings. The success of
the act did not exactly surprise me, though it had
never crossed my mind, earlier in the evening, that
the girls would fall for each other in such startling
earnest, practically on first sight, or that their

mutual attraction could produce this happy harvest, before one could say Tallulah Bankhead. Casilda, I realised, might perhaps have been feeling a trifle starved for this special form of love, which no doubt meant more to her than she was prepared to admit. Bless her wicked heart, I couldn't blame her for getting up to her old tricks again so soon, at the drop of an eyelid! But, casting my mind back over Janet's case history, I did not recall that she ever showed much liking or aptitude but rather, on the contrary, a natural distaste for any hint of these naughty digressions, which I would, I confess, have been only too ready to encourage and approve. It was obvious that Casilda had taken the initiative tonight, and was calling the tune, but I was equally fascinated to see that Janet must have welcomed her overtures without the faintest hesitation of demur, judging by their present harmonious pitch of enthusiasm. There had not been time, after, all, for any lengthy process of persuasion, and Casilda, with her unfailing sixth sense in sexual matters, had clearly neither delayed nor rushed the pace unduly. They seemed meant for one another – and both were bent on proving it.

I crossed over and sat on the arm of the sofa. Casilda's black jersey dress was off one shoulder. She had undone Janet's shirt and removed her bra. Between them they struggled to get her out of her tight tartan trews. Casilda signalled to me for aid. She had slithered on to the floor and delved deep into Janet's lap at once, leaving the upper half of the long, slim body in my care. Janet's rosy limbs were flung wide across the cushions, like a starfish stranded helpless on the shore. Hers was the emaciated, abandoned carcass, we the plundering crows that swooped on her in unison to gnaw her vitals. Neither of them at last could bear the strain another moment. Leaping to her feet, Casilda wrenched off her sombre plumage, quickly cast the layer of downy silk beneath, and, launching the full force of all her naked weight into the saddle, bestrode the eager mount that bucked, quivered, reared, bounced hard up to meet her with a wild, savage will of its own. I was thrown off my perch and was forced to relinquish the tiny, tender, dancing tits to Casilda's strong grip, as she seized them for reins and clung to them also for support while she rode the cleft of Janet's crotch, hitching it fiercely to her own, twisting and writhing against it, plunging, pressing, thrusting more and more closely, more deeply into the devil's dripping mouth, the open breach, the entrance to the loins' dark, leafy-locked, mysterious cave, to dig within its folds on a hot quest for hidden treasure. . . .

I could have sworn that the violence of this encounter made the roughest moments of the frenzied frolic I had witnessed between Helen and Casilda seem like child's play. Among several reasons for this distinct impression were the fact that here was a new and unexpected challenge, that it was largely a novel thrill for Janet, whose physique was particularly well constructed to ensure that she should get the utmost enjoyment out of such an awkward method of fornication,

that both girls were conscious of their appreciative
audience, so may have been tempted to play up
accordingly, and not only had Casilda lately been
deprived of this pleasurable outlet but probably she
felt that, given the chance to cuckold me a little
into the bargain, she must trespass on an ancient
light-o'-love of mine with an extra vengeance. She
did not stint herself, certainly, nor pull her punches.
But Janet was never one to take things lying down
– at least not in any metaphorical sense. She gave
as good as she got, on principle – and in this case
she put up such a gallant show that she succeeded,
with all her wiry might and by a swift, wrestling
eel-like motion, in turning the tables completely on
her more solid opponent. I did not see how it was
done, but in a tangled flash, after a brief upheaval
of flailing legs and humped muscle, the lightweight
came out on top, like a bantam in the cockpit, amid
a triumphant flutter of wings, spurs and waving
crests. It now seemed better so. She held Casilda
in the scissor grasp, and their joint movement, fast
and furious, grew, rose, galloped, pounded, swelled
to Valkyrian speed . . . when the door behind me
opened, and Andrew walked in.

He must have used the back way. He stopped
dead in his tracks and stared at the scene that
confronted him, but said nothing. I handed him a
drink off the mantelpiece, which one of our women
had sipped and left. We stood side by side in front
of the fire, watching with all eyes. Still he did not
speak. I was glad. Only brute force could have
separated them. It would not take long . . .

suddenly there was a single loud, sharp cry from both their throats – followed, seconds later, by a choking, breathless rattle of joy that fell away in the lost, heavy silence. Languidly Janet withdrew, as a man does, quitting the flattened body that has received the gift of his sperm. She staggered slightly and dropped into a chair. I passed her the rest of my cognac. We gazed at Casilda, lying motionless and spent, lax and spread-eagled on the sofa, as uncovered and starkly indecent as a corpse. When she moved at last, and looked at us, it was to clutch at her fork, her throbbing parts, with a quick shiver and a broad, quiet smile; but not to shield the wound or hide her trembling flesh from view. Her playful fingers parted it in fact, lightly toying with the matted curls, stroking the flushed red rim all round, as though applying an oily balm to soothe a gently tickling sore, and skimming down its blatantly bare, gaping length, as in a quick canoe between bushy banks, she sighed, arched her back lazily, with yearning, and rolled her tousled head upon the cushions. We knew what she wanted – a different, immediate and deeper solace. She had made that plain enough.

'Take pity on her,' I said to Andrew, 'since she's asking for it. You have my permission.'

He glanced at Janet, who nodded. 'And mine,' she said.

'No – that won't quite do.' It was Casilda who spoke, to our surprise, as though she could not yet have revived sufficiently to communicate with us directly by word of mouth, but must continue to employ her more expressive sign language.

'Both men – I'll have you both,' she said, sitting up. 'That's it, that's what I want – and always did. Hurry, can't you – get undressed! One in front and one behind. We can manage that if we try. . . .'

It took some managing. Andrew had already torn off his clothes, before I could work out what Casilda meant or how she proposed to set about it. She sat huddled demurely on her tail now, a caricature of modesty, waiting. She studied us carefully although of course she didn't need to examine me, it all depended on Andrew. He was enormous. The tool he carried was a long, gnarled, hefty great club – a bludgeon. I was astonished. Casilda's eyes opened wide. She wet her lips. For such a little fellow, upon my soul, you would scarcely believe it possible – the most lavish endowment, and considering that it did not show up to advantage, under that bulging stomach, frankly excessive, an outsized monstrosity. How women can contemplate such repulsive objects without flinching in horror at the sight, they alone know! It had a curve on it like a rhinoceros horn or a hockey stick – and no less vast were the balls, slung in a hideous, wrinkled sack, as big as a cantaloupe. The corona itself was a dark, bursting ripe red plum, stuck on at the end of a thick, knotted bare branch – nothing short of grotesque. There we were, standing to attention, with weapons at the ready, presenting arms for Casilda's inspection. She leaned forward, putting out a hand to each of us, in an unconscious, ribald parody of a royal command soiree, assessing our offers – medium and immoderate – with judicious concentration on the big problem that faced or otherwise intimately concerned her.

In point of fact the choice was obvious; but she anointed us both for her own ends, when Janet's sisterly perception had sent her post-haste from the room, to the medicine chest, on an errand of mercy. The sofa looked a bit cramped, I thought, for the three of us, but Casilda shook her head when I beckoned her to the wide, woolly hearthrug, and, firmly drawing the two members of her party towards the couch, she lay down on her side, without letting go of us, as we loomed above her, wondering what to do next. There was only one solution, which Janet, the idle spectator, promptly advised, though it probably dawned on us all simultaneously. We turned Casilda on to her back. Andrew got up into position with some effort and misguided vigour, yet not so precipitately as the pawing stallion who needs assistance to put him into a proper fix, oddly enough, rather than to pull him out of a hole – and they settled down to it straightaway, going great guns, hard on the job with everything they had.

It was a sight to see, and thrilling to overhear, for they made the deuce of a noise, rootling like stoats, though neither of them said a word. None of us had a stitch on. A lurid light shone in Janet's eyes, as she hovered and circled around the inebriate pair, like a referee. I hopped, in sheer torture, from foot to foot, torn between fiendish impatience and jealousy. My turn would come to repay this lewd, hot-slotted nympho in kind, and I hoped it would hurt the crazy, cock-struck whore – hell take her grinding guts, I'd give it to the bitch till she laughed on the wrong side of her foul, fat fanny, damn it. I'd shoot some decent good sense up her leching, bawdy bum and fill my lovely lady with a jolt from a prick every bit as rich and randy as his . . . but when? Would they never stop? She was carried away completely, curse her, she had forgotten all about me. He'd spend, and spoil half our fun in a minute, if she didn't watch out . . . ought I to take the risk and cut in? Where was Janet? She'd serve, at a pinch. It was then, praise be, that Casilda rolled over, pushing the chap with her, jabbing him in the ribs, shoving them around, both of them, to lie, still copulating like monkeys, on their sides, with him facing out towards the fireplace, his back against the sofa, and she, in reverse, showing me her buttocks, the white, milky full moon of her bottom turned to me. There it was at last, beaming, big, broad and beautiful, in all its innocence or insolence, bland or crass, according to how one looked on it, delivered into my power as a hostage, meat indeed for the slaughter, rakish and docile, the sinful flesh. . . .

It was worth a further fleeting delay, a moment's scrutiny. I bent over the two-backed beast, ran my hand along the steep ravine between the smooth, cool cheeks, which jounced about distractingly under stern orders from in front, though Casilda thrust her tail outwards as far as she dared, while

179

I probed the pursed little brown buttonhole, like the bud of a tiny wild-flower, with my fingertip at first, and then, flinging myself on the sofa behind her, and prising the massive mounds apart, with an inch or so of the old codger himself. Easy does it, in he goes – just as slippery and sweet as you please . . . no trouble at all – for a couple of split seconds, that is, until we got the warhead in place, truly embedded, streaking up her fundament like a dentist's drill through a temporary stopping, an express train roaring full-on into a tunnel, a bull-dozer boring a trench in a stiffly packed squelch of clay. But then, ye gods, what a to-do! What shrill yelps and yells, what wriggling, tugging and dodging, what tearful entreaties, elbowings, fisticuffs, and ghastly oaths! I held on to her grimly by one hip, with the other arm round her neck, and ploughed on, regardless of the cloudburst, which passed and was gone in a few more shakes at the crucial base of the triangle. . . .

The last of this trio, however, was the first to quit. It wasn't my fault. I had shot my bolt a little while before the others finished – which apparently they did, bringing it off very adroitly, together. I might have lasted out, too, if Janet had not seen fit to chip in as an auxiliary to our already somewhat overcrowded act by prodding me from the rear and swiping at my backside with her open palm, just when we were all approaching the terrific climax of our intricate threefold exercise. It's true that I was teetering on the sofa's edge the whole time, and nearly got butted off on to the floor once or twice, because there simply wasn't room for three on it: Casilda had her arms and legs coiled around Andrew in a ferocious hug to keep him in place, the couch was far too short, we stuck out in every direction like a cactus patch. But Janet's well meant intervention hastened my undoing.

I started to dress, and Andrew was about to follow suit, but his wife would not hear of it. She had snuggled up next to Casilda, cooing affectionately, but her hackles rose on the instant when she saw what was afoot.

'Hey, no you don't!' she cried with comic indignation, although quite seriously. 'That's all jolly fine – but what about me? You two stay right where you are, until I'm given just the same treatment as Casilda here. How frightfully ungallant of you, Tony, to try to sneak out on me, again! Really you're both absolute bounders, I do think. But I shan't allow it! I won't have you make such cads of yourselves. Come here!'

'Janet, honey,' I pleaded, 'have a heart! With the best will in the world . . .' I pointed to my cock. It was shrivelled and limp.

Andrew's, as she could see for herself, was in an even more pitiful plight – shrunk to a third of its former size, it hung down only a quarter of the way to his knees, like a discarded old rope end, frayed and soggy. Ugly enough at the peak of its rampant grandeur, now, in this tatty, slack, bedraggled state, it was simply revolting.

'I'd be no lousy use to you, my sweet,' he protested mildly. 'Another day – '

'Come here!' she repeated. 'We'll look into this. . . .'

We were leaning against the mantlepiece, side by side, warming our backs at the fire. We did not budge – so Janet dropped on her haunches between us on the hearthrug. She refused to lose faith. She was not going to take no for an answer. We swayed, drooping before her very eyes, our crinkled, deflated organs dangling under her nose. She set to, an ardent revivalist, tackling the desperate, double task with both hands. I got the left, her better one – and she took us to task with both hands at once. She was making a lovely job of it, quite like old times . . . soon it was better still: I got her undivided attention, when Casilda flopped down beside her, and took over half the work. Now Janet could devote herself wholeheartedly to doing one thing at a time – too beautiful for words . . . her undivided attention was nothing if not widespread . . . she flagwagged signals to Casilda, reporting progress, while simultaneously she massaged my scrotum and slid a hand between my legs, to visit warmer regions, where a venturesome middle finger went on an expedition to explore the interior . . . Janet was never so rash and clumsy as to frig a fellow at all strenuously until it was required of her. In my present condition, any but the most gradual first aid would have proved fatal. She rubbed and kneaded my testicles, pinching and playing with them, while merely brushing and stroking my phallus, as though to chafe and polish it, with a certain curious maternal fondness, for its own dear sake. Comparing by results – which are, after all, what counts – I'd have said she ran rings round Casilda; but I may have been biased by gratitude in her favour – especially when she went the whole hog and adopted heroic measures, with her tongue at first, then her lips, and finally her mouth, that other vulva, a cavity as scorching-hot and spongy but twice as clever. . . .

We were the more advanced; Casilda was finding it an uphill, gruelling chore to strike a spark into that dormant, mouldy member, so she consulted me with an air of punctilious servility. 'May I?' she asked. I gestured dumb assent. She clapped her kisser like a leech to his gross organ, which had begun to swell and stretch by infinitely small degrees, like some slow-waking giant. There, she had something to be going on with! Personally, my cure was almost complete . . . we looked like queer bookends, the four of us, like heraldic supporters or carved figures, flanking the chimney piece, although the caryatids knelt, shoulder to shoulder, while the quaking male pillars could barely stand upright, but had to be propped and girded, fore and aft by sustained, intimate pressures from below. We were lifted and wired underneath. Andrew and I, to make a peculiar nude frieze with our two ministering angels, the fairer and the darker, identical in their position yet so different in build, the one full-boded and shapely, the other spare and lithe. With heads bent over their labours, noses to the grindstone, their agitated mops of hair were hoisted on our joysticks at half-mast, as though luxuriant, extra fleece had sprouted from his protruding paunch and my pale belly. Casilda linked the circuit by lending a hand to fiddle with Janet's pussy – a bonus which Janet promptly requited in kind. Andrew's arm lay, lightly touching mine, along the mantleshelf.

Casilda took command as mistress of ceremonies, but Janet jibbed at the sofa, like a horse at a hedge, so our tricky threesome was accomplished this time, in the end and with equal or even greater difficulty, after various vain attempts on the rug, when Andrew was shored up with pillows on the edge of a large armchair, Janet impaled herself upon his prong, to sprawl face down on top of him, crushing him against the springs and hitching herself high up into the air for me eventually to perforate at my leisure, though not without some jabbing and incitements from Casilda, who skipped around the simmering stewpot like a witch doctor. My orgasm was the last – a feather in my cap, I thought – and for a few moments after we were through with the smothered underdog, Janet and I shunted to and fro in ecstasy, a toppling pile of flesh, like a three-decker sandwich, that sagged to rest where it lay, until Casilda called us to get a bite to eat in the kitchen, which Andrew aptly compared to a nudist's canteen.

'Whenever you feel like a return match,' said Casilda brightly as we left, 'just let us know.'

CHAPTER NINE

Until she reminded me, I had forgotten that
Casilda's three-months' 'probationary period,' as
she slyly called it, was nearly up. One evening I
told her that I would have to go over to Paris soon
on business. She was soaking in her bath, like a
delicious archipelago gleaming in an ocean of foam.

'I see,' she said, rising Venuslike while I talked
about the trip. 'Hand me my towel, honey . . . I've
been here long enough, I guess. It was time I got
out, anyway,' she added, turning around to hunch
her wet shoulders into the big bath towel, which
gave her the air of a bather getting undressed with
elaborate modesty on a beach.

'You've boiled yourself a fashionable pink, as
usual,' I remarked. 'Luminous but painful to look
at. How you stand it, God knows.'

'Easy,' said Casilda, drying herself in a sequence

185

of unconsciously alluring poses that would have earned a photographer his month's meals. 'I'm in my element when I get into hot water. You should know that, Tony darling. But it's not what I meant, of course . . . oh, well, never mind.'

'What the devil did you mean then?' I was slow on the uptake.

Casilda sifted a white cloud of French Fern over certain parts of her rose-flushed, tawny, yellow-brown self, and eyed me with a half-pitying frown.

'Just that I count on you to bring me back something pretty from Paris. How long will you be away? Can I hang on here for a bit, until you let me know?'

'Do you want to?' I asked, much amused. It had never occurred to me that she might misinterpret my words as a tactful farewell. 'As you like,' I continued, grudgingly acquiescent. 'I only felt that – '

'No, all right then,' she snapped. 'Let's call it a day.'

'I thought you wouldn't care to be left here on your own. I don't need to stay very long in Paris, it's true – but that small attic I share in Montparnasse will be empty for the next couple of months. Margot has gone to the States, as I told you. So I might as well camp there awhile – why not? We could have a good deal of fun in Paris, one way and the other. I was sure you would jump at the chance. Still, if you'd rather – '

'You mean I'd go too? Why in hell didn't you say so, Tony?'

'It went without saying, damn it all! What made you think otherwise? Maybe taking coals to Newcastle, I agree – but I assumed you'd expect to come along.'

'You're a lousy bastard, my good sir,' said Casilda, adjusting the loose toils of a frail suspender belt that dangled from her middle like the feelers of a dead octopus, framing her belly in elastic brackets about the thick, silken splodge of her powdered short hairs.

'You led me up that garden path very neatly,' she admitted. 'But the great thing in life for a floozy is to know when she's wanted – or not anymore. I'm only here on appro, after all. How long have I had to prove my worth? Three months, nearly. I was expecting my congé any time now . . . not that I deserve to be thrown away yet. You've got yourself a bargain here, if you ask me.'

Hands clasped behind her neck, she swung her ripe breasts and revolved her ample hips in a brief, fetching parody of a Turkish tummy dance. I held out my arms, from close range on the bathroom stool.

'Your contract is extended indefinitely, Miss Vandersluys – until we get a colossal bid for you from an oil king or some rival studio who can afford to compensate us decently for taking you off our hands,' I assured her.

With reptilian fingers weaving before her face and an odalisque's hypnotic eyes darting shafts of amorous enticement over her *yashmak* – a chiffon slip draped across her nose – Casilda gyrated onto my lap and sat astride my knees, swaying, wriggling and twirling her arms. She was her master's suppliant slave, but, as such, she took the lead with astute anticipation of my every wish – which in fact she herself created. Needless to say, I was already aroused and equipped to deal with the insinuating houri in summary, straightforward fashion. She would not, however, permit me to do so. A properly instructed harem vamp has more respect for the union rules of her craft. Men are clumsy, ungrateful brutes – but they are capable, if subtly inspired, cajoled and guided, of dispensing to the top of nature's bent the lavish bounties of their wondrous godhead. That is what a girl wants most in all the world, and can have at any time, if she goes about it wisely. Casilda had more recondite uses for my impressive erection than that which had occurred to me ipso facto. The whole thing was taken out of my hands there and then. Bemused and contented, I lent her my tool, and she – humbly, solicitously, with a pretty fair imitation of the resourceful wiles of oriental lovemaking – did the job. I accepted her blandishments as my lordly due . . . the result was that we staggered out to dinner very late.

Lifting a corner of her flimsy makeshift veil, she engulfed my mouth in a lascivious, liquid kiss that pushed me into an almost horizontal position with my neck propped against the wall. At the same time she reached over into an open drawer of the medicine chest for an electric vibrator which I had quite forgotten I owned. Trust Casilda in her leisure moments to unearth so pleasant a toy! She plugged it in, and employed it with stirring effect on us both, before springing up to swivel me around on the stool as a pivot, so that my elbows rested, firmly supporting our joint weight, on the edge of the bath – for she surged back immediately on top of me, with a supple movement, to perch and lie down full length upon my prick. I lay pinned, like a butterfly, underneath her though my role was rather that of a guinea pig in the laboratory or of the heftier partner in an acrobatic act at the circus. Continuous evolutions were performed upon my supine torso by this undulating, improvised nautch-girl, whose gymnastic talents I had hitherto never suspected.

From a swimming posture on my chest Casilda raised herself, curling her legs beneath me, and then, leaning backwards, she lifted them both, one after the other, until her knees were pushed up under her chin, almost touching it, as she huddled herself with a sort of sinuous concentration, clasping her ankles, so that her feet rested in the hollow of my stomach and her heels were pressed against the stretched expanse of her squatting thighs. Motionless she remained at this angle for a moment, gripping and distending the strong inner muscles that held my shackled member within her burning, slippery sheath as in a vase. She had me on the rack, splayed out, recumbent in a levitated luxury of mingled pain and pleasure, a raging contrast of sensations, acute and dazed which she contrived, with a tormentor's dexterous cruelty, to check, reduce, renew or aggravate at will.

Casilda changed her position three or four times, as one chooses a different combination to the lock of a safe. Leaning on my thighs, she uncoiled her long legs and stuck them straight out in front of her, so that my head was flanked to left and right of her shins. She made me hike myself nearly upright, slid us across the floor and hooked her knees over my shoulders to draw me still closer down towards her by crossing her feet again tightly behind my back. My trunk was bent forward, hers leaned away from me as far as possible: we were a couple of oarsmen wildly rowing opposite ways in the same boat. It was not easy skulling – but Casilda increased the strain wilfully, very slowly, with scientific precision, when she undid the knot, pointing her toes into the air above my head, and gingerly worked herself right around on her pelvis – and mine – to end up facing outwards, with her back to me.

It was not until we had completed these elaborate exercises and got ourselves at last into a comparatively simple fix that Casilda consented to discard all caution and gallop through to a passionate finish – yet, even then, she scorned to lean out frontwards in the normal manner, but on the contrary lay back against my chest thrusting me down flat once more until only my nape and bottom were squarely supported on the edge of the bath and the towel-topped wooden stool.

I had investigated all these various clinches before – most of them with Casilda herself as well as with my other concubines in the past – but I cannot recall having sampled the whole gamut at one sitting on any previous occasion, nor ever in such highly precarious circumstances. One is willing to try everything once, of course, or more often – and so are two, I've found, half the time – but really bed is the only place for gallant conjuring feats or sinewy tests of endurance. Casilda's flights of fancy had wafted us through a dizzy, dazzling firmament of stars – but I begged her, when we returned to earth, never more to drag me from the safe anchorage of a mattress planted squarely on terra firma.

Soon after Easter we were installed in my dear old flame Margot's dusty, ramshackled studio off the Rue Lepic, with spring in the air and just enough money to scrape by on for the time being. If we were to have a summer holiday, I had to buckle down to work.

'D'you know what?' Casilda remarked at breakfast one morning. 'I should have a kid sister in this city, some place – if she's still knocking around. I lost track of her a year or two ago. By way of studying art in Paris, she was. Wonder if I can contact her through the old address – or we would certainly meet up with her if we settled at the Deux Magots for a while . . . you'd take to Anne, I think. Very easy on the eye – unless she has managed to ruin her looks by now. She's six years younger than me – a half sister, actually. Her father was a crooner from St. Louis. If you consider me a minx, wait till you see Anne. . . .'

'Barely twenty-one,' I mused. 'An attractive age – but maybe a shade unfledged for me still. . . .'

'Gos, no, not on your life!' Casilda snorted. 'Besides, you're already headed for the pinafore stage, *mon vieux*. Haven't you noticed? A criminal taste for the sweet young things is developing fast, I'd say. How about Cécile, for example?'

'Well, yes, all right, now that you mention it, what about her; oughtn't we call on the little chit at school, or take her out or something, since we're over here? It would be only polite.'

Casilda raised her eyebrows but made no comment. Nor did I. What was there to say? We exchanged looks that might either mean nothing at all or else were pregnant with intentions too iniquitous to be expressed between us in words. I had a sort of inkling that Casilda had come round quite a way recently from her idiotically priggish attitude on the subject of the little Delavigne lass. I would not put anything past her in that line. She was vicious, my darling Cassy, but also and above all she was unaccountable. She had an exceedingly soft spot for Cécile – and now, in addition, there was a keen desire on her part to be revenged on Helen. In fact, she was quite serious about that, unlike me – which wasn't unfunny. She had taken her dismissal by the Baroness with a far more ill grace than I ever expected. Personally, though, I did not feel much inclined to egg her on in her nefarious schemes. The thought of Anne attracted me, but I wasn't particularly interested in the snooty little schoolgirl, who would no doubt yell blue murder and run to Mummy if Casilda or I even looked like touching her. . . .

Or would she? Had I not hit the nail on the head that time when I taunted Casilda about the deceptive quality of maidenly innocence? For all I knew, Cécile might turn out to be a slim little chip off the old block – in which case she would surely take to any necking games we might propose to play, like a duck to water.

That was certainly the opinion I formed one evening when I came home to the studio and found Cécile closeted there with Casilda – in an atmosphere that struck me as charged with strong, peculiar currents of feminine conspiracy, though it was obvious that they had merely been having tea together, Cécile and her mother's best friend, whom any impressionable damsel might look up to with affectionate admiration and envy. In Cécile's adolescent eyes Casilda must have appeared as a glamorous film-star, an elegant lady of fashion, a worldly-wise companion and a sweetly condescending older girl, all rolled into one

Our pretty visitor was just about to leave when I arrived. Her manners, as always, were perfect; she thanked us both for the lovely time she had had and looked forward to coming to this picturesque pied-à-terre again, if asked. I could see that Casilda had not glossed over but rather stressed the carnal nature of our relationship, which stood out a mile, anyhow, in the restricted lebensraum of the studio, so that, without overdoing it, she had been able to give the teen-ager a discreet object lesson in the happy art of living in sin – not by a sordid display of crumpled bed linen, but by a bohemian profusion of laundered underclothes strewn about the place to betoken an easygoing state of conjugal intimacy. Casilda hastened to explain this gaudy disarray.

'It looks like a naval occasion, I know,' she said. 'We're dressed overall with bunting – but that was done for Cécile's benefit. She was crazy about my 'mass of nice things.' I'm afraid I encouraged her. I've been modelling this whole pile of nonsense for hours – and sent her off with a couple of my naughtiest numbers as a gift. Her eyes were popping out of her head. I wished you'd been here – you'd have adored it. She's really an absolute honey. I shut the bedside table drawer and pretended to hide one or two whatnots which it wouldn't be good for her to see. She was desperate with curiosity, of course – and she blushes most becomingly! I was itching to kiss her – but it was better to go slow and win her confidence. I've made tremendous progress . . . by the time tea was ready – or rather, port and pastries – we had broken the ice to a powder, I can tell you, and began to let our hair down in earnest. We are as thick as thieves now. For a well-brought-up kid, primed by her mother not to unbend an inch in any direction. I must say she's amazing. I gave her a few shocks, which were a big treat for her, I guess – but they helped to draw her out beautifully. She knows it's ill-bred to appear inquisitive – and she would die, as you can imagine, at her age, rather than let on that any aspect of sex might still hold some mystery for her, except from actual experience and practice. She thinks she has the whole thing taped, theoretically speaking. I dropped several veiled references that properly foxed her, but she never made a slip or shot a line or balled up her understanding manner in any way. It was a delicious conversation. She is no faker and no fool. She's terribly eager to learn – though there isn't much fruit left on the tree, to be honest, that she hasn't already spotted, if not nibbled. . . .'

'What did I tell you?'

'You're dead wrong. As her mother confessor I can pass on her confidences to prove to you how pure she is, poor pet, in spite of having been exposed for months to an appallingly corrupt influence out of St Cloud, my dear . . . that's a smart finishing establishment, all right. Cécile is having the whale of an affair, as adult and romantic as you please, with the daughter of a Tunisian sheik. It's a positive hotbed of vice, that high-classed joint. But she is only on the fringe of the ring – probably because she's too scared to join the really fast set. The trouble is that Leila, thè Tunisian, is a lot younger, but she makes the running. She's stuck on Cécile with a true schoolgirl pash – imagine that, on top of a sultry temperament, the seraglio background, a colour complex, what a bonfire! She's Cécile's abject slave and meek, "pi" handmaiden, of course, but an importunate, brow-beating bully into the bargain. If it weren't that she keeps threatening to poison her, I gather Cécile would have cut adrift long ago. She's a good deal more frightened than fond of her dusky chum, and but for that she would probably have achieved her heart's desire, which is to tuck up with an older girl, a Greek named Marina, who sounds to me like the only genuine lez of the lot. She's their Queen-Empress, and her word is law on matters of sex. She cashes in on being a compatriot – if not a direct descendant, naturally – of Sappho herself, and all but the dumbest other moppets stand in awe of her because she was raped, she claims, at fourteen and had several men before she set foot in the place. There's a court of three favourite rose-buds in constant attendance on her. "My vestals," she calls them – a Dane, a Chinese and a Belgian. I reckon she has had her eye on Cécile for some time, but is biding the moment . . . she had sampled and cast off the Tunisian, and takes it out on the Dane, whom the others – I mean the lesser lights – envy terribly, because she too is no longer a virgin. She was seduced more or less in the nursery, and can't see anything wrong with that. Nor can Cécile. The obliging Dane likes it both ways, and makes no bones about it. She is known to have kicked up her heels for the music master and the gardener at St. Cloud – so of course she has the jolly reputation of doing any chap a good turn at the drop of a hat. The upshot of it all is that Cécile is the classic *demi-vierge* – mentally, though she has had no leadings with the opposite sex. She simply can't wait to leave school and launch out on a roaring affair with the first comer – that is, if he tackles it right. She is moderately attracted to Leila, *faute de mieux*. But she is yearning to play a truly female role under a man's rod of iron. Subconsciously it's a lover she wants – and needs. Failing that, for the present – since she's timid and unsure – her great ambition is to make the grade with the Chinese or the Greek. Socially, in her world, that would be tops. She cordially dislikes the Belgian, who pokes fun at her innocence and accuses her of being so terrified of masturbating that she wears rubber gloves whenever she goes to spend a penny.'

In point of fact, the conquest – or, if you will, the violation – of Cécile Delavigne was not such plain sailing as Casilda had led me to expect. For Casilda, of course, it was easy enough – a simple problem of seduction – but I had to use force. I didn't mind that especially – it added a bit of incentive, in a way, to an otherwise fairly dull adventure – only the thing was I hadn't envisaged any difficulty, and it came as rather a nasty shock to me. I do not look back on the episode now with any pleasure. Doubtless the silly little fool couldn't help it at the time – but she hurt my feelings considerably, blast her, so nobody really enjoyed the incident, except Cassy.

It was a fortnight later that she fetched the girl from St. Cloud to spend the day with us – her main idea being to catch a glimpse of the famous Marina, I surmised, and some of her young ladies-in-waiting. I was out to a business lunch – with a book at a bistro round the corner. I let myself in as noiselessly as possible, and neither of them heard me, though I recognised the sounds all right, from

197

outside the door – the low, sweet, unmistakable rumble of lovemaking. I tiptoed across to the curtained alcove and leaned against the wall to listen. What soft music of delight in the ear, not only heavenly and divine but of this world of earth, the battle hymn of the flesh – starry music of the spheres the deep, rich, endless melody of sex – ah, harken to its strains once more, how blissful a duet to sing, how good to hear it sung! I scarcely could capture what was said – a word, a phrase at most, amid the muted, whispered murmurings, between the strange, long intervals of pregnant silence, broken now and then by a faint, quiet sigh, a louder, sudden, sharp intake of breath or the hurried, urgent, glad confusion of speech that bursts like a torrent, like a hot shower, upon the excited eavesdropper's brain, fretted by the mysterious, intermittent, barely audible tune of rustling bedclothes, creaking springs, bodily movements or by an occasional brief sequence of muffled, plaintive, incoherent groans, which ends abruptly, as though the torturer had gagged the victim with a kiss.

The sound track was familiar – a transient, lovely recording which I knew by heart but never could hear too often, nor carry in my head, because this is an intricate ditty, a part-song calling for two voices, and always, to strike a fresh, gleeful harmony, they must be new. Casilda's gentler tones, with their slow, clear American cadence slurred to a more husky yet caressing pitch, were dominant most of the time that I waited and trembled, holding myself in check, for a cue to release me from purgatory. When I peeped round the curtain, they were locked still in each other's arms, with heads on the pillow, almost motionless, while lower down, at the centre of activity under the blankets, their intertwined, cuddling limbs sent now and again a dense volcanic tremor rippling and heaving up to the surface. There was little to be observed at this initial stage of the proceedings – but the slightest disturbance would, I knew, prove fatal. I retired and contained my impatience with a *fine à l'eau*, and then undressed without a sound, donned pyjamas, and gazed out of the window at the view, while keeping both ears cocked towards the ladies' annexe.

Curiosity at last got the better of me – yet my entrance was perfectly timed. Casilda's twisted features greeted me with a grimace of only partial, pent-up recognition, for the writhing, naked, top half of her body was largely obscured by the coverlet which rose and fell in a flurried, scrambling hump across her middle. The hump, roughly female in shape, was her invisible companion, who was dragged up from the depths after a while by Casilda, to reappear – somewhat reluctantly, I thought – like a diver. Blushing scarlet and flushed from her exertions, she looked, I have to admit, unspeakably bewitching. Casilda embraced her fondly, stroking her hair, her nose and brow, and as they lay back in bed, the pair of them, exhausted, stretched out like half-waked cats, glossy brown and gleaming black, their slight or ample curves outlined beneath the sheet pulled up to their chins, they formed a picture of such beauty that it would vanquish the heaviest sorrow. . . .

I stood there smiling at the sight, at my own good fortune, at both the girls so snugly abed together, and at each in turn. But the instant Cécile's drowsy, faraway eyes focused on me, they went wide with alarm and were filled with embarrassment and shame. She gave a little gasp – 'Mr Grey! Oh! Oh dear?' – and buried her face against Casilda's shoulder, under the blankets, as though she were still an innocent child, and even butter wouldn't melt in her tender young mouth, let alone the honeydew briny tang of sex.

'Why is he here?' she bleated feebly. 'You promised me . . . it was us two alone – our secret. He was never going to know – you promised me that. You did, you did!'

I sat down at their feet on the divan, thoroughly nonplussed and crestfallen. Casilda tried hard to soothe her little pal – she talked, she argued, pleaded and cajoled. She besought her to see reason, just to be sensible and calm. Everything was fine, it would be all right, she'd see, if only she wouldn't take on so. Now, really, what was this stupid fuss about? Why could she not be gay again, and kind and sweet, as she was before? At first Cécile's misery seemed to grow worse, but in the end it looked as if she was persuaded. Enough, at least, for me to slip between the sheets by her side. She even cheered up sufficiently to sketch a nice, meek, rueful smile. I attempted to make light of the whole thing as a merely silly, trivial misunderstanding. For a time I did not touch her. I chatted airily, affably, quite aimlessly about this and that . . . it was best to leave the next move to Casilda – whose capable hands began, very gradually, to work wonders. Cécile stirred – uneasily at the start, imperceptibly almost, it was the tiniest wee twitch, she was determined not to squirm. The flesh was weak, although far from willing. I smoked a cigarette, got up to fetch us all a drink – just coffee for Cécile, she said, which I laced with brandy, dawdling over it, while I could hear them whispering to each other. . . .

'I've explained to this darling, foolish poppet of mine that you simply want to watch us, that's all,' Casilda reported, 'when we're like we are now, so close and cosy together . . . she's adorable, Tony. You mustn't be angry with her. It's such a cute, wonderful – oh, heavens, *umph*! – delish person. And, honestly, what a body it has – bless it! You never saw . . . I'm going to make love to her a little . . . she's my own good, dear, marvellous sweetie-pie. Look – take a load of that!'

She flung the clothes off for me to see, and I caught a glimpse – a miserly fleeting glimpse – of girlish nakedness, before the crazy, cringing little nincompoop grabbed them and cowered herself up again to the neck.

'Oh, no, please! He mustn't!' she squealed. 'really he mustn't!'

I might have lost my temper there and then – but at a warning glance from Casilda I managed,

with an effort, to control it for the present. I got
back in beside them, but refrained with the utmost
stoicism from all physical contact with either the
nitwit pupil or her admirably industrious teacher.
I sulked, in fact, while Cécile bristled with nervous
hostility or suspicious caution, and Cassy did her
stuff. She did it well, as I had foreseen – superla-
tively. It was not long before she had stoked the
fire to a white heat. She had the hypocritical young
hussy tossing and thrashing on the five-yard line in
next to no time. . . . Cécile gurgled and spluttered
like a burst pipe. She did not know what she was
saying or doing – or whom exactly she had to thank
for what she was feeling. She moaned, she cried,
she frankly howled for more – more! She entreated
us not to stop, never ever stop. I took her at her
word, now that she had changed her mind. I was
devouring her tits. Glorious they were – hard,
round, small, juicy and pink, like apples. I can't
say, of their type, when I've tasted better. I was in
love with my work – deliriously happy. Casilda
wasn't letting up, either. She was down there,
guzzling away, gulping like a pig in a trough,
feasting on the girl's slimy-spiced innards, hammer-
and-tongs, putting her heart and soul into it, the
gluttonous bitch, with all the gallant tenacity of a
bulldog. I had the corner of one eye on her the
whole time, it was fun watching her. Even then,
with the three of us wallowing in our excitement
like lunatics, my sense of humour nudged me,
mentally jogged my elbow, to point out a ludicrous
detail: she was a film star advertising some common

brand of soap or cosmetics, her priceless, ideal countenance defaced by a guttersnipe's jest with the inappropriate addition of a thickly scrawled, twirling black moustache. In the circumstances I considered, all the same, that Cécile's lustrous fungus suited Casilda's style of beauty, for, as a silken, hirsute, androgynous adornment of her mannish upper lip, it was perhaps not entirely out of place. . . .

Her thoughts, it seemed, ran parallel to mine. She wanted more definite offensive action on that cracked front than even she could offer. Cécile's clinging arms were linked about my neck and shoulders, to prevent me from abandoning her bosom. Casilda's free hand was frantically engaged in stiffening my morale for the assault. She knew, only too well, my sudden limitations, my maddening aptitude at the last moment for turning tail . . . this was no easy hurdle. I must be whipped past the sticking point, but yet not overshoot the mark. Disaster loomed ahead, if we failed through faulty timing . . . we were coming up to it now – a trifle too fast? She gave me the high sign, sending me off with a slap on the bottom. It's all yours . . . I got what she meant, I sprang up, as she rolled out of my way. She sat back on her haunches and in one quick movement pulled a pillow down under the girl's arse, lifting her squarely onto it and tugging the legs to either side, wide open, completely apart, as far as they would go. . . .

What screams! What an unholy hullabaloo! I was chilled, panic-stricken by the noise. I thought she was having a fit. I couldn't say when or how, but I let her go, eventually. It was beyond me. I did my best. I fell flat out with all my weight on the struggling, shrill, raucous bitch, I pressed and thrust and butted and pushed. I pinned her claws back out of my eyes, I muzzled her with my mouth. I did what I could to wind her, to keep her quiet – and Casilda helped. Casilda was a tower of strength. But there was nothing for it. I had to give up. I had pierced her slightly, the merest fraction. She wasn't even bleeding, though. Anyone would have sworn, I had deflowered her with a carving knife, to judge by the shindy she raised, the cowardly, snivelling, prudish little clot.

She sobbed and shuddered, she wept and whined and implored me to let her dress and go away. She used her tears – most unfairly – to retaliate and choke me off when I endeavoured to reason with her. Well, there it was. We sat around, the three of us, dejected, upset, baffled. Alternately she kept up a stony silence or babbled excuses and apologies in a repetitive rigmarole: she was sorry, it had been too much for all at once; no man had ever seen her stripped, even, until I'd been so rough and cruel and horrid to her just now; she couldn't help it but I must be kind and have patience; why wouldn't I wait a little longer, because bit by bit, maybe, later on she might, after a time, in a different way, only not yet, not straight off like that; she was a virgin, and it had hurt terribly, dreadfully, she hadn't realised, she had no idea, though, of course she did know it would; so if I'd promise to be more gentle, when I asked her again, but now, please. . . .

'No, no, please no,' she droned. 'I can't – and you simply mustn't. I won't. Please not. . . .'

Did I have to lecture a grown girl on the harsher facts of life? I was too tired . . . in the rare previous cases when I'd come up against this minor but irksome chore of domestic surgery, the patient had the decency not to involve us in a distressing scene of futile tears and recriminations.

'It was for your own good,' I warned her, 'and you would be well-advised to take a hold on yourself and get it over, pretty soon – unless you want to end up a pathetic, desperate old lesbian like your mother.'

I suppose I should not have said that, although it was true: I wasn't thinking.

She blew up, sizzling with fury.

'What d'you mean? How dare you? Filthy, dirty beast! Anyway, you're far older than she is – old enough to be my grandfather, you evil lying brute!'

She clobbered me like a wildcat, scratching and screeching. I was too taken aback to defend myself. My lip was cut very painfully, and I could hardly see out of one eye. In a flash she leaped out through the curtains.

She had got most of her clothes on already when I caught up with her and hauled her back into the alcove. That was all right by me – it meant tugging her skirt off and fighting to pull her knickers down. Or were they Casilda's? No, they fitted those twin perky young pumpkins too smoothly and neatly, dotting them simply with embroidered specks and enhancing the general presentation with the sweetest blue bows at the side. It seemed a shame to remove so dainty a dish cover . . . but Casilda held her flat while I bared the rotund, cute, plump, childish bum of the Mademoiselle. Damn the rampageous, highborn little savage – she had whetted my appetite by her antics, she needed correction, she had it coming to her, she was in for it, to spare her would be to desist from my obvious duty. I did not weaken, I took a long-handled clothes brush to her. Severe chastisement, I grant – but it had the most salutary effect, in opposite ways, on the pair of us. Scarred and softened, roused and rampant, we were more attuned now to each other, properly equipped and receptive – or at any rate acquiscent. The rest was comparatively easy. We rolled her over, and Casilda rained kisses on her face and throat while I drew her down into position, half off the edge of the bed, lifted her knees towards the ceiling, and splayed them out at convenient angles, as the executioner steadies the block or widens the noose for his victim.

Cécile uttered a single piercing howl then she fainted clean away – which perhaps was fortunate.

Casilda brought her round, and nursed her, I'm sure, with the utmost solicitude, when I mooched off. To fill in time, I went to a movie.

CHAPTER TEN

Neither of us bothered anymore about it, until the
letter from Helen arrived, bearing a Paris post-
mark. I thought after the event that I had maligned
Cécile, but here were my previous fears all too
grimly confirmed. She had squawked to her mother
straightaway, the shoddy little sneak. Helen needed
to see Casilda urgently, at once, the letter said.
Cécile had written to her in terrible distress and
'has told me all!'

We were glumly pondering on this pretty kettle
of fish when the depraved young so-and-so herself
rang up, in a dreadful state of penitence and
confusion. No, she couldn't talk right now – but
she had to explain, they simply must meet 'before
you talk to Mummy.'

'I've already heard from her,' Casilda replied.
'She wants me to call immediately at an address in

the Rue' – she glanced at the writing – 'Passy . . .
oh, you're there too, are you? She has taken you
away from school? No, I shall get in touch with
her tomorrow sometime . . . yes, that's what she
suggests. I gather you spilt the beans, and told her
everything . . . all right, come around here, any
time . . . yes, but I can send him out . . . oh, very
well, but what's the use? Do you know? Then it
wasn't awfully fair or sensible of you to give your
mother the wrong ideas about us . . . you didn't?
Are you sure? How much does she know in that
case? I don't follow. Cécile! Listen – Cécile!'

'She hung up,' said Casilda. 'Helen even talks of
putting her into a convent – imagine! But it seems
she kept quiet about us – me and her at least – in
her S.O.S. to Mamma. You got the rap all to yourself, my boy – not me! Our little fling is our own
precious, safely guarded secret – though I'll bet
Helen guessed it, knowing her. I wish I could figure
just what the story was – I'll have to get hold of
the girl and find out.'

Casilda did not telephone Helen next day –
which was lucky, for two reasons: we got word from
Janet, and Cécile hung up again, charily, Janet's
news was very disturbing: she felt she ought to
warn us without delay of the evil gossip she had
picked up casually, from mutual friends, over cock-
tails. It appeared that for weeks now Helen had
been spreading the most fantastic and atrocious
slanders about us in London. She had assured
anyone who would pass on the tidbit that I fled the
country with Casilda because I was wanted by the

police for criminal assaults but of course Casilda had left me, for a Negro pianist, as soon as she discovered I was impotent and only got any pleasure from being unmercifully flogged – a whim which she was willing to indulge, at a price, until she got bored with such repellent, insane habits when I tried to turn pimp and live on her immoral earnings in Hamburg.

Jane's report made Casilda spit with fury. 'Helen is off her head,' she decided. 'How could she invent such foul crap about me? I'll get her guts for this! Malice is one thing, when old chums fall out – but this is downright calumny, and it stinks. She'll be sore and sorry after I've rubbed her nose in the shit! You're going to help me, too.'

Cécile's call was timely. She pressed again with quavering anxiety for an interview. 'I've dropped Helen a line to say I'll go round there about six o'clock, Sunday,' said Casilda. Oh, then couldn't she make it a wee bit earlier, Cécile begged, because Mother would not be back until that time from a visit to the elder Delavignes, and she wasn't keen on taking her along 'in the circumstances,' so Cécile would plead a headache or something and stay at home to wait for Casilda, who coldly agreed. 'That'll be lovely!' Casilda described their meeting to me afterwards. Cécile received her with tears of contrition, a gush of excuses, and open arms. She had a lot to say that was muddled and unimportant, but her mind was made up. 'I was as stern and ungracious as possible,' Casilda declared, 'but she led me straight through to her room, babbling fifteen to the dozen all the way and trying to kiss me, like some slick, hulking sherwolf, and before I knew it, there I was, flat as a pancake on her maidenly couch, with my skirts over my head and that young trollop was sucking me off, fit to beat the band, as if this was just what the doctor ordered. Okay, my child, I thought, get your snub little snootful, now that you're at it, while the going's good. There was no stopping her, anyway – so I did my level best to last out long enough for Helen to come in and catch us red-handed. Can't you picture the scene? Wouldn't that have been perfect? As it was, the smart kid covered up all tell-tale traces before Mamma arrived – but I strolled out of the love nest, tidying my hair and purpose-fully plying a lipstick. . . . Helen wasn't going to be drawn, though. She ignored the ugly hint completely. It didn't suit her to quarrel with me, apparently – she had other ideas. The conversation started quite calmly, on the most normal note. I let her take the lead. She didn't expect to be taxed with her lies about us, I could see it rather shook her – but she denied them flatly. That is when we began to get a trifle heated. "Don't shout so!" she kept saying. I had cottoned on to the game by then – she really and truly hoped to win me round! We assumed she would be full of fire and breathing threats like a dragon, didn't we? Not at all! She never came out with it in so many words – but, believe it or not, she was ready to forgive me! She would take me back, and let bygones by bygones, if I'd throw you away at once and return with her to London! Oh, yes, and Cécile, too, I suppose. Think of it – how extraordinary! – I lost my temper, I'm afraid, at this point – so she sent our innocent witness out of the room. To spare her blushes! "Go and lie down, Cécile – Cassy and I have to talk things over. Don't interrupt us till I call you – in a little while. . . ." Of course after that I led her on. I changed my tactics – slightly, not too, blatantly. I lit a cigarette and took a drink. "Very well then, Helen," I said, "let's have it out, heart to heart. Why do you hate me? Because I like sleeping with Tony, or because I won't go to bed with you anymore, since you've taken against him? It's your own stupid fault, you have to admit. We gave you the chance – remember? – that night when he fucked you – " She sprang at me then. I had gone too far. I had used a rude word – and mentioned your name, in the same connection. I made to defend myself, all the time I'd been waiting for this attack . . . but I was wrong. Murder was not – obviously not – her intention. I struck her quite hard in the face as she leaped upon me – but her arms were round my waist, and as I was knocked off balance by this cannonball in the midriff, and fell backwards into a chair, she smothered me with kisses. She always was a passionate bitch, but now she was starved, incensed and crazy . . . I repulsed her as roughly as I could, with a slap that sat her down sobbing on the floor at my feet. We remained like that for a while . . . she had gone all to pieces. I looked at my watch. You were due to arrive any minute now, the way we'd timed it. So I spoke to her – just to see what she would do – a little less gruffly. "Off you go," I said. "If you want me that badly, get undressed." "Why? Don't make fun at me," she sniffled. "You don't love me . . ." "I'll show you how much," I told her. "But only this once – and no more, ever again; it'll be the end between us." Of course she couldn't understand or believe such a drastic ultimatum. "What about Cécile," she asked. I dared to taunt her – "Afraid she'll be jealous?" I sneered. It was too easy. I waved her out of the room. Helen, of all people! No shred of pride, no comeback, nothing. . . . She swallowed even that indignity. "Shoo!" I said. "Cécile won't mind – but we'll lock ourselves in. . . ." I waited a few minutes, left the front door ajar for you in the hall, went through to Helen, who was there naked on the bed – and the rest you know.'

The rest was a cannibal picnic, with Helen as the pièce de résistance. Casilda as high priestess of the cult, myself – the chief slave-trader – presiding, and Cécile served up as a tender green salad on the side. We did not invite her to the party, although she was mainly responsible for cooking up this whole mess. She nosed her way in, during the second course, when it got pretty rowdy – so she had to take the consequences of her spitefulness, curiosity, impertinence and deceit. She'd have raised the alarm, and made trouble if we had let her go. Casilda kept her promise. She allowed Helen a thorough good inning – without a murmur, as if inert submission to the labours of love was not the

response Helen expected, at least it gave her a
candid, bitter reply to her question, as well as the
opportunity she so desperately desired. Cut to the
quick, she rebounded her frantic efforts, cherishing
without stint the flesh of the beloved, only to beat
her brow against a blank wall of relaxed, almost
comatose indifference, which drove her so nearly
out of her wits that I arrived to find her digging
her nails into Cassy's flanks and pummelling them
with her clenched fists.

My entry broke up the sensual farce with the
melodramatic denouement of a veritable deus ex
machina. There was no need for a word to be
spoken. Helen could have died on the spot from
surprise. She gazed at me as though I were a ghost
– a ghost with a horsewhip – and at the bedroom
key clutched to Casilda's hand, which showed her
that she had been bamboozled. Like a rat she was
trapped – and like a snake in the grass she tried to
slither into cover next door. But Casilda seized the
slender small body, slung it back struggling onto
the springs, and grappled with it fiercely, lashing
and twining in naked warfare as silent and sinister
as the mere hiss, thud and cracking of twigs in a
fight between a python and a cobra on film.

It was an exciting parody, in reversed positions,
of their previous embrace; they shifted and tumbled
through varying holds and poses, and as a carnal
display of the female physique from all angles, one
could not have wished for a finer spectacle. I sat
entranced at the end of the bed, pouring over this
album of bawdy snapshots which was being shown

to me like an illustrated catalogue of strength and beauty, a rare production that would have warmed Andrew's heart, I reflected, as much as mine. Not for the world would I have interfered to call down the curtain on such a lively and lovely ballet. I had come to this place as Casilda's ally. I was there to help her, with the allowed purpose of seeing that justice was done, that it did not miscarry. But Casilda herself was the avenger, the actual executioner; I was the solemn judge. It was she who felt so strongly about Helen's outrageous affronts to our honour. I meant merely to ensure fair play – and to take a hand in it perhaps, at some later stage of the proceedings, if the spirit moved me to act. At this point, I swear, I was content, as the onlooker, just to watch. . . .

It was a foregone conclusion: the odds against Helen were too heavily weighted, she did not stand a chance. I was almost glad, from the sporting point of view, when reinforcements turned up for her in the wild shape of Cécile – a flying column in a flowered cotton housecoat – who burst upon us, altered now by her mother's cries, as if to rescue her in the nick of time. Casilda had forced her disloyal friend flat down on her face, I had tossed her the riding crop, since she was clearly the victor, and holding the slim bare back securely in place, with a knee on the nape of Helen's neck, she was about to thrash the living daylights out of her. The first couple of whams had landed at whistling speed with a dull thump that was instantly drowned by a shrill scream, which would echo too loudly

214

through a respectable neighbourhood; though it was music to my ears, I cast around for some gag to stifle so strident a sound, or mute it at least to a more refined note that might pass for enjoyable revelry in the 16th arrondissement since Helen's own was evidently beyond protection . . . it was then that Cécile popped up – and flew at me! At me, the linesman, minding my own business! I shoved her off into the melee, where she belonged, the silly twat. She only upset everything, got buffetted about, all mussed, torn, scratched and womanhandled – and came bouncing back to me out of the scrum, straight in the pit of the fly-half's stomach. I spun her around and held her fast, with her elbows pinioned behind me so that, bent up close against her, I had the willowly little body with its jutting, pneumatic buttocks pressed to me tightly, moulded on my codpiece like a fruity plum pudding. But the meddling brat had knocked Casilda arse over tit, Helen slipped through her fingers, cutting loose in a flash of greased lightning across the room – and when she turned, glaring at us from the corner next to a chest of drawers, there was a revolver glinting in her hand.

It was a tense moment. Luckily Cécile happened to shield me in front to some extent – but she was woefully slight, there was scarcely anything of her. I was much the taller of the two, and had it not been for Casilda's mad, foolhardy impulse to fling herself forward in a headlong angry rush on Helen, wrestling the gun from her grasp, I might not have lived to tell the tale. As it was, Cassy emptied the pistol and we breathed again – but Helen wasn't joking, there was no damn doubt about it, that was certainly a very narrow shave.

Helen only had herself to blame. My blood was up now, the ugly fright she had just given us made me see red. I cheered and shouted encouragement to Casilda when she bundled the dazed Helen back onto the pillows, stuffed a nightdress into her mouth, and laid it on thicker than mustard, larruping the hide off her until her arm grew tired. I pushed Cécile nearer from the other side of the bed, to get a better look, and could not resist tipping her down over the edge, crossing her wrists across her shoulder blades, so that I had it all just where I wanted it and in two twos, with a mere flick of the hand, prettily exposed. This time there was no difficulty – at least I noticed none, or next to none. I backscuttled the girl at my ease, as she lay across the downy, facing Helen – and a glorious pair of martyrs they made, mewling, quivering and sprawling together like blind kittens in a basket, while we both exerted ourselves to the utmost, determined, while we were at it, that the lesson should sink in.

Yet it seemed to me that Cassy's vengeful rage soon burned itself out, for after roughly a score of strokes her whip hand wilted. Then she was struck by a brilliant idea. She rummaged in a drawer. 'I thought so!' she said. 'Always totes this around with her – our darling gadget. Never say die!' – and she produced a realistic rubber replica of the male organ, the hugest, toughest-looking dildo you ever saw, with leather straps dangling from it, which she affixed in a trice, changing sex automatically, with the great threat erected between her hips, like a flagpole or an ack-ack gun planted on a mound of golden gorse.

'Ladies and gentlemen,' Casilda proclaimed 'I am pleased, nay, honoured to inaugurate this splendid and expensive subway, which I hereby declare open for public use.'

Without further ceremony she rammed the monstrous contraption home in Helen's cunt almost jolting her upright on that hefty lever in the process. I had my work cut out to prevent her raising the roof and to keep her, like a captive balloon, from snapping her guide ropes and sailing away into space. This exciting tussle made a new man of me, though – and once I had quieted her down a bit. I managed to deal with Cécile in similar, simultaneous but much milder fashion, vying with Casilda in an orgy that reduced us all to mincemeat before we had done.

'Well, we put them through their paces,' said Casilda. 'Let's go.'

It was safe to leave them now: they would not, be getting up to any serious mischief again for a while. So we scrammed. The sullen, damp drizzle chilled us in the Rue Passy.

CHAPTER ELEVEN

There was method in our badness. Operation Vineyard had been planned beforehand in detail: it covered one hour of reckoning with the Delavignes, our prompt departure from Paris, and the sunny southward trip to start our summer holiday. I was in funds again, we were taking Sister Anne with us, Casilda had been loaned a villa by the sea in Spain on a generously indefinite lease, everything in the garden was lovely. To hit the road in the Citroën was like riding the crest of the wave.

The hideout we were headed for was a film star's weekend residence that belonged to her director-husband (number three) a former pal of Casilda's and a sweeter sugar daddy than most. Her rollick with him during her first marriage probably owed its success to her having played, for once in her life, hard to get. It was among her least humdrum experiments, and when we ran into him at Maxim's with his wife, the exquisite, dumb, pampered Gloria Gilmour, he recognised his old split with genuine relief and gratitude. That single sentimental reunion may have sufficed to work the oracle (as Casilda always doggedly maintained). I don't rightly know, but in view of how much talk there was, when we joined them at dinner, about 'this Spanish bungalow of Gloria's that's just going begging,' I prudently made myself scarce the next couple of nights, because if Paris was worth a Mass, it seemed to me Putonas was a fair swap for the trifling loan of a temporary poacher's licence. Schminsk himself ('call me Milt') had picked the place up for a song, he explained, but would be filming in Italy till August, though Gloria might drop over to relax between contracts maybe ('she's off my hands, on Sid Cleanfart's payroll'), which should suit us all okay, he guessed, as the cottage was plenty big enough – it had everything and was kind of cute – so they would both be very, very happy to have us utilise it, anytime. 'Rope in a few houseguests,' he advised; I'd sure hate those lazy dago servants not to earn their keep.'

Anne naturally headed the list. Later, as there were six bedrooms at El Delirio, we hoped the Mackenzies would come to stay with us awhile. But for the present, after the trying, long winter, the prospect of two or three months of utter idleness in the heat, under clear blue skies on the beach or in the scented shade of the pines, had us cavorting and chortling from sheer joy all the way. We had shaken the city's dust off our heels, which soon would sink into pure sand, a load of worry had slipped like a halter from our necks, and for full measure, to top perfection, there was Anne – life was beginning anew.

No problem at all, our little sister, but a fascinating, bright fresh page, one that I had not turned to date . . . it made my mouth water to think of the journey ahead, the moonlit nights and drowsy, sunfilled days, the torrid siesta, the naked, baked prostration, gasping with the gorgeous sweat of sex, that alone stirring, burning, full-blooded, wine-fortified, real and rampant within the dark secrecy of shuttered rooms. We had run Sister Anne to earth only the week before – and here we were now, launched on the wings of adventure, with a ravishing, romantic idyll in the bag, bound for a treasure trove on distant shores that stretched away in vistas of delight. The moment I met Anne I had said:

'She must come with us – we'll take her too.'

'We will, too,' Casilda agreed. 'Sure thing. We two will take her – no?'

Then, after a thoughtful pause, she added: 'I never have . . . but I don't mind the idea – of being half-incestuous. She's only my half sister. There can't be so much wrong with that.'

She read my unspoken query.

'Oh, her – she won't care,' Casilda said.

Nor did she – not in the least. Casilda was right, as usual. Anne made a heavenly change from some other stuffy punks I could mention. There was nothing of the tough swell dame about her, either.

In every way, down to the last and most personal particulars, she was no Gloria, and she had nothing, so as you would notice, in common with Helen or Cécile – or even Janet. A wholesome trollop – gay, good-natured, and vastly entertaining. As unspoiled as a spring flower plucked in a woodland glade, as refreshing as a gin fizz or the brine-laden breeze, as plump as a partridge, sweet as a pigeon – and promiscuous as only the devil or she herself could be. She had beauty, youth, health and high spirits, with the humour and the unconscious charm that goes with them – the amoral animal quality which even Casilda's gay temperament, lacked, or had lost with the years. Here was the milk of human kindness in purest form, on the counter, nourishing, creamy and curiously good – in limitless supply. She was admirable as well as adorable; no man could help liking her.

Anatomically, for my taste, she was perhaps just a shade too buxom, and I preferred Casilda's less vivid, more subtle colouring – but with her poster curves and her brilliant vitality (a 'vulgar appeal,' Helen might say, as distinct from 'sensual allure') it was clear that Anne, like her sister, would look better for artist-friends as a model – and at Putonas we both intended to paint. Anne was a corn-yellow blonde, where Casilda was merely fair-skinned, and the fur of her pussy was deep orange, like some cats' – or marmalade thickly spread in a triangle on buttered toast.

That breakfast relish I discovered betimes – on our first stop for the night. We dined superbly, and on our cheerful return to the hotel, Casilda slid an arm round her sister's waist, as we climbed the stairs, asking point-blank: 'So which is it to be, toots – cock or cunt?'

Anne actually had the grace to blush – but she found the choice altogether too hard, as one might have known, and plumped in the end for both. A born good lay in her own right, she erred if anything on the side of excessive zeal and impatience – a fault in the right direction, as nobody will deny – and showed herself never averse to learning a few special, invaluable extra tricks of the trade from her sister's wider experience. The teacher-to-pupil relationship was a source of happy amusement to me during our Spanish journey – and it may have saved my bacon, what's more, because Casilda's tuition gave me a much-needed rest now and again, whereas without such peaceful intervals I might not have survived the first carefree month of our triangular exertions. Anne – bless her warm heart and even hotter you-know-what – soon became something of a handful which, single-handed, would have floored me for the count.

I hit on a grand solution, however. Jeremy, my son at Oxford, would be the answer to a maiden's prayer and a middle-aged man's problem. He would leap at the chance of such a stunning vacation, little knowing what he was in for. It was arranged by cable that we should collect him off the train at Jodete. I hardly recognised the lanky, solemn yet engaging youth, with his good clean looks, his slight shy stammer and his sedate air, as my own small bastard whom I had not seen for years. Nobody would have said that his mother was the sassiest Irish barmaid I ever met. We tried to liven him up over a healthy lunch at an inn on the way back, with lashings of rough red wine. Jeremy had a strong head, but I despaired of his ingrained diffidence. We drove off into the sweltering afternoon, with the sun overhead like a blowtorch. Casilda was dozing, bare-legged, on the rear seat. Anne, for some reason best known to herself, had elected to squeeze up in front between Jeremy and myself when we set out again, though she would have been more comfortable, as before, sitting at the back with her sister.

'She wants to snooze,' Anne explained to me confidentially, and at once dropped off into an oblivious, somnolent state of digestion, herself, with head lolling, crucified arms stretched out behind us, east and west. After a while, with one hand on the wheel, I laid the other on her knee, started to stroke the left thigh, slid gently tapping, probing, skating fingers under her pleated grey linen skirt, and dipped them into the thicket of soft brambles that guards the hidden, brackish well of love's delight, the spring of life itself. Anne's adoration of the sacred mysteries was not by any means a secret or a selfish cult. Opening her legs, she welcomed the intrusion with as glib a grace as if no tourist had been admitted past the turnpike to visit this famed grotto during the recent 'off' season. That I knew to be untrue. But I was not alone on the excursion. Pretending at first not to notice, eyes fixed straight ahead into the glare, Jeremy hovered. He fidgeted, gulped, his mouth was dry. Anne stretched and mumbled, settling herself at ease, but did not wake. Emboldened faintly by her tact and a broad wink from me, eventually his hand started up the smooth path in gingerly pursuit, on the opposite side of the gulch, timidly following the beaten track, yet venturing after my lead no further than about halfway. We each had a leg to ourselves, but I was already waiting, though not idly, at the crossroads, where, if only he would join me, we could divide the spoils to everyone's greater satisfaction, including Anne's. He did not want to gate-crash, to go too far. He stopped dead, or lingered and kicked his heels, then crept forward again, testing the terrain as cautiously as an advance patrol, not a mere forage party. He was a very raw recruit indeed, new to this front, evidently, but guided by an old scout he did his duty like a man and ended the campaign a credit to his instructor. Meeting me up there at last, entrenched athwart the tiny milestone, he pushed along the low road while I took the high road, dividing our labours in a combined, two-fisted operation, for as he vigorously frigged her quim, I tossed her off, lightly rubbing her clitoris with my most gentle touch. We blended our endeavours to perfection – basso profundo, pizzicato – and were rewarded by so delirious an ovation that Casilda awoke in alarm, crying: 'Look out! Careful – damn you, Tony, pull up!'

Anne was already madly vociferous over her enjoyments; you could hear her coming for miles around. She copulated altogether like a jungle cat. I braked in a patch of shade, and she was gone almost before the car halted, tumbling out at once with Jeremy into the sparse, dusty clump of trees by the roadside. Casilda smiled. 'Quick off the mark,' she commented.

'It's amazing,' I said, 'but, d'you know, I think the boy is a ruddy virgin . . . at nineteen!'

'No! Well, for Heaven's sakes! Ought we to supervise?'

'It would probably put him off his stroke. Anne can cope. He'll be all right.'

But we went in the end. Curiosity got the better of us. And he was far from all right. They seemed to be making an awful mess of it. Even through a thick carpet of pine needles, the ground was baked hard. He had cleared some away, but the place was littered with rocks and thorns. 'Maybe scorpions, too,' Casilda remarked cheerfully, in a hollow tone, squatting beside them. Anne, flushed and grimly silent, was near to tears. He was sprawling awkwardly on top of her, his shirtails fluttering, but otherwise there was little movement. It was a sad picture. Both were half clothed, looking dirty and crumpled. His face was distraught, and pouring with sweat. Anne's head was turned to show a scowling profile as she stared at some insects scurrying among the stones. He must have wasted a great deal of time to reach this piteous stalemate before we got there, without apparently having progressed at all. It was a plain case of premature ejaculation, one could tell that at a glance. Poor chap, the excitement she had provoked in him by the novelty of such yielding, unabashed sexual contact in the car had burned his fingers, yet when confronted with the gaudy flower of the open female flesh, known to him solely by its sticky touch, his blood ran hot and cold in waves of sharp desire, sick shame, fear and nervous haste. By waiving the romantic preliminaries of a delayed approach to what Swinburne calls the 'foliage-hidden fountain-head' itself, the crazy, cocksure tart had unmanned him with the unadorned revelation of a tremendous gift that took his breath away. No doubt he strove to tarry awhile before entering the haven that was both a refuge and a whirlpool in one, as he well realised – only to foul the shallows, a buffeted and broken wreck on his maiden voyage. He had blurted out his brief, pretty speech too soon, and now remained there, quaking, a piteous victim of stage fright, unable to withdraw. . . .

Casilda went to the rescue, without demur. She rolled Jeremy's loose-limbed, doleful corpse, like a shot rabbit's, to one side, and flopped down next to him, after folding his trousers as a bolster which she wedged beneath Anne's bottom. For me, in my frisky condition at that propitious moment, it was an opportunity not to be missed. While Casilda fiddled with the young fellow's pathetic, conked-out periscope, seeking to repair it to the point where he would get a less glossy view of life, I ripped off my pants, and also Anne's sports shirt and bra, which robbed me of the view and feel of her exuberant bosom, whetted her appetite again by knocking at the door very formally for admittance, then shut it tight behind the visitor by crushing her fat thighs together on my bullocks – like lackeys huddling outside on the porch – and topped her soundly in that position: the double nutcracker.

Casilda was making up to Jeremy for his sorry debacle with solicitous care, and the lucky blighter profited most emphatically from both her frank hand-to-mouth treatment and the object lesson that Anne and I laid on for him, with several interesting variations, at close range. Casilda allowed the callow youth to reciprocate her kindness to some extent – chiefly for his own sake, as an indirect means of speeding his renascence and bringing him up to scratch. He watched us deep in coition, goggling with envy, and gesticulated to convey his readiness to require the services that had pulled him around, hand over fist, by pleasuring Cassy there and then. He would have wallowed all afternoon in that dingy copse, which was an oven, thinking to stuff Casilda first and have enough spunk on tap for Anne when I got through with her. A boy's bravado! Why weep over spilled milk if there's plenty more to be had for the asking? His effrontery infuriated me, such fantastic assurance was unbearable! Yet I was to discover during those next few weeks something I had forgotten since I myself was his age – that Jeremy's ever-readiness to tumble a dame at any time and just as often as he chose (once he caught the knack of it) was no empty boast or flight of ambitious fancy. What he lacked in finesse (he had none) as a lover, he could supply without stint in activity between the sheets; call it mere manpower, rather than stamina – it produced much the same result in the long run. The short, sharp bash was his speciality, and his stock of such fleeting favours appeared inexhaustible, which suited Anne, and others like her, truly down to the ground. His impudent pounce on Casilda was not rebuffed but eluded; he was fobbed off by her uncommon talent for masturbation. 'Not now, thank you, Jeremy dear,' she smiled, as a long, thin thread of his seed spurted, like a rope of scattering pearls, over the stubbly soil. 'that will do to go on with. Between us all, we'll make a man of you tonight. . . .'

There was a wire from Janet at the house: Andrew could not get away, but she could come out alone for a bit next month. Anne was in a somewhat disgruntled mood still, which was extremely unlike her, and she complained morosely that we needed a couple more men, maybe – he-men – but certainly not another skirt around the place. An argument started between the two sisters, whose nerves twanged like guitar strings, and was kept up as bitchily as possible through evening drinks and dinner. I was deeply flattered, for it was plain to be seen where the trouble lay; now that I had lassoed Jeremy into the party, Casilda and I obviously would be tucking up on our own again, leaving Anne to do as best she might with this almost beardless boy of mine. She rebelled against the arrangement, which struck her as grossly unfair. She couldn't expect Cassy to give me up or consent to take Jeremy on in part exchange, and the thought that our gay little threesomes were already over, almost before they had begun, sent her round the bend with disappointment and wounded pride. She felt she'd been tricked, and claimed we were lousy, inconsiderate heels, guilty of deceitful discrimination in palming her off on a stranger. Misguided as it was, her attitude showed she was nuts about me, and Casilda bore out this highly complimentary conclusion when, strolling down to the sea, behind the other couple, for a midnight dip, she assured me that I was more than a match for any young puppy she had ever encountered in the lists of love. 'There's no pro like an old pro, darling,' she said. 'It doesn't take much to deflate one of these boisterous whippersnappers, soon as look at him. Jeremy is sweet. Give him time. But cheer up – if I ever go in for baby snatching, I'll loiter around the pink cots, I expect, not the blue. Maturity is my motto – in men and wine.'

This touching testimonial lifted a load off my mind. Jealous pangs had assailed me already, at this early stage of our happy holidays at El Delirio, and I cursed myself for overlooking the potential dangers of a tricky situation when I summoned Jeremy so blithely to my aid, I had thought only of securing a measure of relief from Anne's exhausting demands, but stupidity did not envisage the likelihood of the boy wanting to sample Casilda's charms as well – which doubtless he might prefer, after tasting and comparing the two lays. It would be devilishly awkward if he pressed for a swap-over, snaffling my girl and landing me for keeps in that other promiscuous floozy's arms – or even if, more reasonably, he insisted on the general family principle of share and share alike. Four might turn out to be a lot worse company than three. On the very first day that the kid showed up – until Casilda quelled my fears – I got a nasty feeling that I had put my foot in it.

I need not have fussed at all, as it turned out. Everything went swimmingly. I mean that we swam, Casilda and I, to the raft moored in the middle of the bay – and there, glistening in the moonlight like fish awash on a slab, we came upon the youthful pair still swimming, as you might have said, in different styles, back stroke and breast stroke, on the sodden matting-covered planks. She had broken him in – that was abundantly clear. They paid no heed to us, though afterwards we all struck out for the shore together, chatting easily, when they were through with their thumping, noisy, rather less hurried poke, and there, lying naked in the sand dunes, they elected to stay a little longer under the stars, while Casilda and I trailed off home.

Later, Anne made a pretty gesture of amends, looking into our room to kiss us good-night. She yawned and, as she stretched, her bathrobe swung open, like curtains, to reveal that flaming orange patch that now shone lighter in shade against her beautifully bronzed, toasted body, smooth and gleaming like a freshly painted hull, with the two dark scarlet beacons topping the summits of the hard, high, rounded hills, the small speck of her navel – and here and there a deeper stain traced by someone's brusing bites at her throat, abdomen and thighs.

'Know what?' she said. 'I'm – hmm! – as happy as those sand-girls you read about, folks. Oh boy, have I had a coupla grand fucks since we all went for that lil' swim!'

I did not object to Casilda exciting the boy on occasion: it amused her as a pastime, and I saw no harm in it, if he craved any extra solace or the added spice of variety. So long as she stopped short of actually getting herself screwed by him, I let them monkey around to their hearts' content. We frequently joined forces, so to speak, or hopped back and forth between beds. It was ideal for me: I had Anne whenever I wanted her – not often, but sometimes during the siesta hour, on a walk through the woods, at night by the water's edge, and once standing in the sea, with her back pressed against a rock and the waves lapping up to our chins. . . . We had just finished a quickie before lunch, I remember, the day Gloria arrived. That was on a bench in the hall, because the maid, Conchita, was laying the table, Gloria narrowly missed stumbling over us. She had not announced her visit.

I paraded my party straightaway, while she was changing, and read them a lecture on seemly behaviour now that the lady of the house was our guest. 'Lovemaking will be strictly confined to our bedrooms,' I ordered, 'and grinds outdoors must

231

take place beyond earshot.' We lived model lives from then on – which was just as well, for I soon discovered that the famous film-star's icy temperament utterly belied her luscious, captivating looks. Gloria Gilmour was as cold, glossy and blank as a coloured picture postcard of some exotic beauty spot. By repute among her fans she was one of priceless wonders of the modern world. The figure (36–24–36) was perfect, and she displayed it freely, all too generously, with innate cruelty and practised grace. Every pose was studied, sensually intoxicating, obnoxiously refined – but if one could tear one's eyes away from the tantalising, scantily clad marvel of her physique, the divine, unearthly radiance of that pure and lovely face was still more blinding to behold. In the sultry seclusion of her palatial home at Putonas this sacred goddess, the idol of a million male moviegoers, walked about in next to nothing but her make-up. Yet, incredible as it seemed to me – and also, as I subsequently learned, to Jeremy – she was frigid. She gazed right through you with a huge, uncomprehending, cowlike stare if you so much as tried, by any possible means of approach, however devious, to mention or even hint at the subject of sex. The very fact of the mating urge did not exist for her. The mind within that platinum dome was two-dimensional – like her bright image on the screen. The gorgeous, natural, palpable shape which she inhabited was merely the mocking, transient reality of a dream. I made several earnest passes at it –

totally in vain. She never noticed. She moved away and talked of something else, or left the room.

I was so puzzled that I took Casilda into my confidence on the matter. She had reminded me that Janet was due next day. 'I can't see those two hitting it off,' said Casilda. 'Not for five seconds. It's a pity we mustn't let ourselves go at all, with Gloria in the house. I was looking forward to quite a bit of fun with Janet. We could have had a hell of a fine old orgy . . . listen – I have an idea. There's a big bullfight on tomorrow for the fair at Jodete. Why don't you take Gloria to it? Tell her it'll be good publicity for her to be seen ogling a matador, like all the other Hollywood hoodlums.'

'Jeremey's going,' I said. 'That's better still – he can escort her. Though, as a matter of fact, she's an absolute iceberg. I'm positive that the only portion of her anatomy that we haven't been shown just isn't there. Between the legs she is made the same way as a statue. She's not normal in the least. I believe she is not a woman at all.'

When I had finished telling Casilda my woeful tale of failure, she burst out laughing.

'Tony, how funny you are!' she gurgled. 'I had never given it a thought – but I guarantee you're wrong. Maybe she is undersexed – but if you passed her over to me, I'd seduce her for you. I don't suppose she has ever tried it with a woman – but she detests men. You can tell at a glance she has never fallen for anybody. She's not a virgin, of course – except perhaps where us girls are concerned. And even so, I wouldn't be too sure . . .

233

she'd need a lot of rousing, and someone to make love to her, getting nothing in return. I might have a shot one of these days. Is it a bet?'

Jeremy got Gloria off to a fairly early start, and we three plodded up from the beach for a late Spanish luncheon in time to save a famished, waiting Janet from collapse. Before dusk, between the afternoon sleep and the drinking hour at sunset, we showed Janet around and bathed. Casilda was overjoyed to see her again and quite shameless in selling the pair of potential lovebirds to each other, as though licking her lips at the prospect of piloting them both into bed with us at truly indecent speed. I felt obliged to chide her for pestering Janet.

'Sure, I'm slavering at the mouth,' she replied. 'I can't sit still. You don't mind how frank I am about it, do you, Janet precious? Since Jeremy has been with us, we've been as hetero as the dickens, of course, and – oh, come on, let's skip dinner. Tony, tell Conchita the ladies are too tired to eat. . . .'

In fact we had an excellent supper, but did not linger over it, though Anne and I took our coffee without undue haste. I lit a cigar.

'So long,' Anne suddenly said, and vanished.

I allowed her five or six minutes by my watch before going in from the terrace. The two great tawny cats had Janet's lean carcass stretched out across the broad, bare expanse of sheet, and were gobbling her up alive; her whole body shuddered slightly, or at times shook with a deeper spasm, the knuckles of one fist were rapping on the clenched

234

teeth between the grimacing, twisted lips of a tragic mask, a mask of exquisite pain, while the other hand clutched now at arm's length the empty air, now at her own or someone else's tresses. The staring eyes in a head that rolled from side to side were fixed on space, and the faint, continual sound that issued from her throat was the soft, dying, querulous bleat of some exhausted animal. I drank in every detail of the scene with an avidity to equal that of the pair of officiating sisters, whose cleft behinds, like lunar landscapes, vast, glowing, smooth save for that one dark central furrow, presented themselves both to my caressing fingers conveniently enough in their kneeling posture, if I spread my arms wide. . . . Anne's turn came next, and I was making free with Janet's boyish rump when the headlights of a fast-moving car swept round a bend on the coast road and shone in through the window. The others were back! Fortunately I had not yet undressed, but only had to do up my fly.

Gloria was alone. Jeremy had met some friends, who would drop him off on their way home, they did not know when – but later. She had left them to their own devices. I could guess what had transpired. Gloria, for her, was almost ruffled – while looking outwardly as cool as ever.

'These Spaniards!' she snapped. 'That bullfighter attempted to paw me! Where are the girls?'

'In bed.'

'What, already? It's not eleven yet. . . .'

235

'Our friend Janet has arrived, you know.'

'Does that explain it? I'd have thought, on the contrary, you would all have stayed up later perhaps than usual. . . .'

'Well, no. . . .' I edged along the terrace. The noise in our room echoed in my ears. She would not be listening for it, of course, but any time now, I was afraid, the sonorous Anne (what rotten luck – wouldn't you know it'd be Anne on the rack at this moment?) might raise the roof with one of her blood-curdling shrieks of pleasure. I must muffle her somehow, before that happened. I turned to dive indoors. 'Goodnight,' I said.

Gloria followed me. 'Don't go,' she almost pleaded. 'Stay here awhile – if they're all asleep, at this hour.' Her tone was petulant. 'Listen, I know he'll be along, I couldn't shake him off, he's after me – that awful bullfighter, Jeremy's soul mate. I refused to dine with them. But he is bringing Jeremy back to serenade me. He swore he would, and that I couldn't resist him. They mustn't find me here alone. I'm frightened.'

'But that's ridiculous!' I scoffed. 'If Jeremy picked up this matador fellow, and made a chum of him, and they got drunk together – well, all right, what of it? We will send the Spandiard about his business pretty quick – and I'll deal with Master Jeremy in the morning.'

'You don't understand. There are dozens of them – his troupe or something.'

'Well, then look here – let's wake the servants.'

'Conchita and the old couple? They're no damn

use. No, the only thing would be safety in numbers. A bunch of us – foreigners, aloof and superior, a group of aristocratic foreign ladies. That'd keep them in their place. I must get those girls up. They'll have to help me.'

Before I could stop her, deaf to my entreaties – and deaf also to the fully audible psalm of Anne's raving pleasure. Gloria strode along the passage, knocked at two doors, opened them, and found both rooms empty. She turned to me accusingly, with an incredulous, perplexed look, biting the ripe cherry of her lower lip. I jerked my head towards the sounds emanating from farther down the corridor, and led her gently to them by the hand.

Probably I was as surprised as Gloria to see the trio lying there in a row, as good as gold, with a sheet drawn up to their chins. They may have heard our footsteps outside, and evidently they were resting between rounds, but in any case the sight of the three innocent heads on the pillows, if one ignored the tousled, matted hair, the flushed, smeared faces, the feverish light in the eyes, made a quaint, comical, appealing impression of a some- what salacious fairy tale or into the senior girls' dormitory. Gloria's impeccable features, that oval countenance resembling beauty's permanant image in a mirror, reflected only sheer bewilderment as she and I gazed down in silence at the three prone, shrouded figures laid out on the bed, as it were for our inspection. We were surveying the snowy mountain scene, with its high peaks, soft slopes and hollows, from an aircraft on a night flight thousands of feet above those mysterious, lofty ranges in the stillness of the moon-filled room. No one spoke. An introduction seemed called for. I ought to say:

'You have not met Janet Mackenzie. This is the famous Gloria Gilmour.'

Instead, on the impish spur of the moment, with the sudden speed of a conjuring trick I whipped back the sheet to uncover the three naked graces, and swiftly rounded off their sleight of hand by hoisting a whole forest of waving legs in the air, like the circus trainer who puts his team of prancing horses through their act. Hey-presto! There – I had shown her the very gist of the matter. She could take her pick. What more could anyone ask than this ravishing choice of targets? Like a barker at the fair, I was inviting Gloria to view the special attractions of my private, astounding, magnificent booth, the original, the authentic Aunt Sally. I catered to all tastes. Where was the gourmet who would turn up his nose at such an array of ripe red fruit so prettily set in charming nests of dark and light and yellow moss?

Helen's dainty black and white – perfect of its type – was absent, out of the running; but Gloria's palest golden loveliness would complete my colour scheme most admirably. All these bodies were brown, with no discordant note among them: only in shade and shape did they vary with that bounteous natural variety which the connoisseur of the nude seeks, appraises and values, as the salt of the earth, in his collection of masterpieces. Visually, Gloria's stunning contribution would make the four-in-hand a marvel beyond price, a bouquet beggaring all description. She would top the bill, wiping the floor – I hoped – even with these notable rivals. Here Venus stood at my elbow – *hors concours* – while Juno, Minerva and Psyche lounged on the bed, awaiting the judgement of Paris.

There was an unbearable interval. Gloria hesitated. I was tongue-tied. The others did nothing. It was better for me to efface myself – but somebody must put a stop to this appalling impasse of coyness and confusion.

'You're safe here from any visitors, Gloria,' I said. 'The girls will protect you. But you should be naked, too, like them. They want to see you as you really are.'

The call to duty before an audience worked like a spell. Automatically, calmly, the complaisant Gloria threw off her voluminous lime-green stole, unfastened the low-necked raw silk dress that matched her tan, and emerged from wisps of lingerie, as a snake sheds its skin, more dazzling than a candle flame, and as bare – except for a cache-sexe the size and colour of a fig leaf. This object, in the expectant pause that followed, she made no move to discard. Uncoiling with insolent languor from the bed, Casilda knelt up, plucked at it inquiringly, and drawled:

'What happens under that thing? Are you shaved?'

The fat was in the fire now, in every sense, and the fur flew. Not that the baffled, bullied Gloria put up much resistance. Morally and physically she

239

was overwhelmed. Casilda snapped her G-string and pushed her, struggling wildly, into the scrum. She went down like a ninepin, and though for a time she tried to escape, protesting and wriggling, shouting and straining. I noticed that she fought cleanly, gamely, without resorting to violence. Not once did she kick, scratch or bite the milling bodies that enveloped her in the fleshy toils of their fiercely lascivious embrace. Janet took the least active part in the scrimmage; hers was mainly, like mine, a watching brief, though she weighed the scales in the two sisters' favour by helping at times to curb, quiet or comfort the progressively less reluctant victim of their unsparing ardour. Gloria's strength of will was sapped, it began to weaken, ebbing away under the ubiquitous pressure of the attack, which drained from her all sensation save that of intimate, increasing surrender. Casilda's persuasive tongue was licking her into shape. The odds were with the big battalions. Gloria's soothing defeat was inevitable, and she accepted it, when it came, in the spirit of a deliverance to be celebrated with a thankful, almost victorious clamour.

The truce did not last long, however. I, at least, if not Casilda, had misjudged the peculiar sexual proclivities and foibles of our hostess at El Delirio. Hers was a split personality. Chilly and unwilling undoubtedly she was – but Casilda had found the only way to her heart. Once roused, there was no holding her. She was a lesbian masochist. Women she loved, but she wanted them rough. It was seldom that she got what she wanted: they were all

too kind. In her calling she dared not risk disfigure-
ment – but she longed to be hurt or at any rate
mauled, dominated, overpowered. Men's brutality
disgusted her, and everything else about them; she
spurned and despised the swine. I was kept at arm's
length that night. I scarcely managed to lay a finger
on her – except in the thick of the fray. For it was
a white night with a vengeance that continued until
dawn – an untrammelled orgy whose vivid
succession of separate episodes would fill a book.
Yet how could one separate them? My wearied
member loses the thread of events in a tangled
skein, a topsy-turvy, rough-and-tumble heap of
twitching bodies and jerking limbs, in a crazy,
flashlit sequence of clinches, as those four insatiable
females tussled together, grunting, gasping,
cursing, groaning, and always changing sides, with
first one, then another gaining the upper leg. No
sooner were Janet and I making love to Anne, after
that first bout of theirs with Gloria, I remember,
than Gloria fell upon Casilda, athirst for revenge
. . . that is how it started – and it ended, long hours
later, in a five-flowered daisy chain, a ring-around-
a-rosy that ran, I think, head to tail, like this:
Casilda – Gloria – Anne – Janet, and me. . . .

Yes, that indeed was the end, little as I guessed
it at the time. We fell asleep where we lay, on the
bed or the floor. But there wasn't room for us all
– not for comfort. It was too much for me. I am
not as young as I was . . . I went and tossed down
somewhere else, undisturbed. Conchita woke me
the next afternoon. There was nobody in the house.

They had all gone, she said. The villa El Delirio was empty. Only my car in the garage – they had not taken that. Casilda and Gloria had left together, and Jeremy had eloped with Anne – in Janet's Sunbeam. And Janet? I asked. Oh, the new senorita had departed with my great namesake, Antonio Carajo, the matador, the Lad from Jodete.

That was seven months ago. I am alone now – still alone. But it can't last. I did have a sort of little affair with Conchita – quite a pretty girl, though simple. She stripped well . . . of course it won't last. How could it? Casilda will come back to me. I know she will.